IF YOU SEE KAY HIDE

QUINN GLASNECK FIONA QUINN
TINA GLASNECK

If You See Kay …HIDE is a work of fiction. Names, characters, places, and incidents either are the product of the author's imagination or are used fictitiously, and any resemblance to actual persons, living or dead, business establishments, events, or locales is entirely coincidental.

©2017 Fiona Quinn and Tina Glasneck
All Rights Reserved

Cover created by Chandell Aikman Sites

Publisher's Note:

Neither the publisher nor the authors have any control over and do not assume any responsibility for third-party websites and their content.

No part of this book may be scanned, reproduced, or distributed in any printed or electronic form without the express written permission from the publisher or author. Doing any of these actions via the Internet or in any other way without express written permission from the author is illegal and punishable by law. It is considered piracy. Please purchase only authorized editions. In accordance with the US Copyright Act of 1976, the scanning, uploading, and electronic sharing of any part of this book without the permission of the publisher constitute unlawful piracy and theft of the author's intellectual property. If you would like to use material from the book (other than for review purposes), prior written permission must be obtained by contacting the authors at FionaQuinnBooks@Outlook.com and Tina@TinaGlasneck.com

Thank you for your support of the authors' rights.

We dedicate this book to naps - thank you, kids, for sleeping!

CHAPTER ONE

BEN JOHNSON WAS DARNED CUTE. As I thought that, he looked over at me with a lascivious smile and winked. Yup. That did it for me. I was going to show Johnson and his *johnson* a very good time. He rolled his police cruiser to a stop at the top of a hill, protected in the shadow of the wall surrounding the old cemetery. Not the most romantic of spots, until you considered the full moon that shined through the window and glinted off Johnson's badge. And seeing that badge was as romantic as I needed. Or wanted.

He slid the gear into park and released his safety belt. "It's good to see you again, BJ. It's been too long."

"Too long?" I wrinkled my brow and let my gaze travel from his eyes down his body and let it rest on the sweet spot framed by his police tool belt. I popped my gaze back to his and batted my eyelashes. "Is that really possible?"

Zoop. Even in the dim light, I could see his eyes dilate to black and the blood race from his face southward.

"I...uh..." He shifted around a bit, adjusting his trousers

to make room for his enthusiasm. "I thought I'd done something to upset you. You weren't calling anymore."

"You were dating someone. And even if it was just casually, I don't play with other girls' toys. You know that. Free-range officers only. And only if they're *very* good." I released my own belt and turned to him. "As I remember it, you fit my second criterion nicely." I let my fingers follow my necklace down my low-cut, fitted blouse.

His gaze was glued to my progress as I played with the pendant dangling between my breasts. He slicked his tongue around his lips. "Good," he said. "I really like spending time with you, and I hated to think I fucked up."

"You don't want to fuck *up*?" I asked as I unbuttoned my first button.

He swung his head back and forth but kept his eyes on my fingers as they moved to button number two. "No. Especially not with you."

I worked my way down to button three. "Not with me?" I asked, pulling the fabric to the sides to show him my pretty little lace bra. I ran my finger along the pink ribbon. Up and down, up and down. "What direction do you like to fuck with me if not up?"

His eyes popped up and caught mine. Held. We both broke out laughing.

"Nice one," he said.

The radio was squawking with officers' call numbers and information about the 911 emergencies coming in. It was music to my ears. Better than Marvin Gay. Johnson reached over and picked up the hand set, then leaned in and kissed me. It was a hello kiss. And then, it was a *hello!* kiss with lots of tongue. That definitely got my engines purring. Yup, there was nothing I liked better than going for a joyride in a cop car while the engine cooled up front—

and absolutely zero relationship baggage packed in the trunk.

He held me tight against him, shot me a raised eyebrow, and put a finger to his lips. He depressed the toggle. "Officer 940."

"Copy, 940."

"I'm taking my dinner break. I'm pulling off on the north gate of St. Clemmons' Cemetery. I've already picked up something to eat." His eyes danced with laughter as his gaze caught on mine.

Holy moly–did he just say that? *Zoop*. I had my own libidinous rush.

"Copy. 940 is unavailable for routing," the communications center said.

He reached behind him and shoved the handset back in place while he pulled me tight against his chest.

"You have something to eat?" I giggled as his lips found their way to my throat. "That was well played."

His hand slid into my blouse and cupped my breast. "Oh, the ball's not even on the court. I'm just sidling up to the field."

"You're pretty good at this."

"I aim to please."

"Thank you, Officer Johnson. Carry on."

And he did. Whew! Did he ever. I was so glad that Ben Johnson was single again. I had almost forgotten about this particular skillset of his.

We wriggled ourselves into the backseat, where things heated up. The nice thing about the temperature rise was that the steam coated the windows and gave us an extra layer of privacy. No one could see what was going on, unless, of course, they saw us giving the shocks a stress test. The not-so-nice thing about things getting steamy was, as it turned out, while others might be unaware of us, we too were unaware of others.

The sudden knock on the driver's side door froze us both in wide-eyed surprise.

"Officer?" It was a man's voice.

I tried to push up off Johnson, but he held me tightly to him. "You're almost naked," he hissed. "Stay down."

The knocking sounded again. "Officer, it's an emergency."

I scuttled onto the floor and pulled my bra back into place. With fingers shaking from a mishmash of hormones, I struggled with the little buttons of my blouse.

"What's the nature of the emergency?" Johnson asked as he wrangled himself back into place and hurriedly zipped his pants.

"Sir, the Death Eaters are back in the graveyard. But it's a full moon."

Johnson pushed his hips up and secured his tool belt. "Do they usually not come out on full moons?" he asked.

"No, they come out whenever they can get to fresh meat. They don't care about the moons. It's just that the unicorns *do* come out in the full moon, and I'm afraid there's going to be a terrible battle. Good against evil. Epic shit, man."

I clapped a hand over my mouth to hold in the laughter.

"Are they here yet? The unicorns?" Johnson asked, doing a final wardrobe straighten. "Stay put," he whispered toward me, then popped the door open.

"No, officer. But I'm guessing its nigh on midnight. That's when the unicorns usually show up. Especially on the first night of the full moon."

"There's more than one night of full moon?" I heard

Johnson ask from the other side of the window. I slid onto the seat and fished around trying to find my panties.

"Three nights. Each full moon they come out and romp in the cemetery. Yes, three nights in a row. They're beautiful creatures. Just graceful and lovely. Horny little things. I'm guessing that's when the girl unicorns go into heat. I'm not sure about the boy unicorns. They seem to be in heat, too. I mean, it doesn't seem to me that unicorns care what sex is joining up with what sex–it's kind of a free-for-all."

"In the graveyard?" Johnson sounded like he was doing his best to keep his tone respectful.

"Yes, sir. But the Death Eaters are down there having their supper. I've been tracking them. Keeping an eye on things. Can't tell you how glad I was to see you pulling up."

"Someone's having a picnic?" Obviously, Johnson thought the man had seen something. Now, Johnson was trying to redefine that something for the guy. Maybe he'd move on, and we could get back to the show already in progress.

The steam was beginning to dissipate, and Johnson angled his body to get between the man and his line of sight with me. I, on the other hand, made use of the mirrors.

The guy who stood next to Johnson's six-foot frame was several inches shorter. His grey hair was scraped back into a greasy ponytail. He wore a bandana tied around his forehead. His body was thin, his face weathered, and his clothes were mismatched tie-dye from head to foot. He was certainly festive-looking. And high as a freaking kite. I wondered if he realized he had a doobie behind his ear as he chatted with the good officer.

"Well, sir, I guess you could call it a picnic. Either way. I've got to find a way to stop a war from breaking out between the unicorns and the Death Eaters. The herd will be here any time now."

I looked where the guy was pointing, but a cloud painted over the moon and everything just looked bleak in the distance.

"Alright, I'll tell you what I'm going to do." Johnson sounded like he'd bought into the scenario and was strategizing with the guy. "Death Eaters come out at night because they hate light and sounds, so I'm going to put all my lights on. Especially the red and blue ones. And I'll put on the sirens. I leave it all lit up and maybe you can keep an eye out and see if the Death Eaters don't leave."

"Yes, sir." The guy saluted.

Johnson popped the front door open. Cops disengage their interior lights so they can get in and out of their vehicles without alerting everyone they were there. I bent over though, to stay out of view.

Johnson reached in and flipped some switches. The whole area came to life with swirls of color, blaring horns and sirens. I watched the hippie dude pat Johnson's arm and say something in his ear. He wrapped his fingers around his doobie to hold it in place while he sunk into the low crouching run of a soldier; and just like that, he jogged out into the darkness.

Johnson stuck his head in the window. "This should just take a sec. He's gone on recon. He'll let us know if this is working."

"What do you really think is going on?" I asked.

"He's high as the Himalayas and hallucinating. We know him, though. Marley. He's a good guy. A Vietnam vet. He's self-medicating for PTSD. We cut him as much slack as we can."

My brows drew together. "You can't get him some real help?"

"I think this is going to be as good as it gets. He doesn't trust Uncle Sam. We haven't been able to get him to the VA." He turned off the siren.

"How long with the light show?"

Johnson checked his watch. "I'll give him ten minutes. The siren can piss off the neighbors. I don't want backup to show up."

"I can't find my panties," I said.

"Oh." He reached in his pocket and pulled them out, handing them to me.

"Souvenir?"

"Just thought you'd want to keep them from off the floor – you wouldn't believe what happens in the back of this car."

"Thanks," I reached for them as Johnson turned his head.

He shut the door as Marley trotted back up to him.

"What did you find?" Johnson asked.

Marley scanned the terrain as he answered. "They've dispersed, sir. They got everything back in place at the grave, as far as I can tell."

"Outstanding. Are the unicorns here yet?"

"Not yet, sir. I think it'll all be fine. Thank you for being here. Thank you for driving the Death Eaters away."

"My job is to protect and serve."

They shook hands and Marley lopped off. Regular gait - no more stealth mode. Johnson opened the front door and flipped off the lights. "Let's just give it a second and make sure Marley heads back to his place."

"He lives around here?"

"In one of the mausoleums. The family knows – they

said to leave him alone. Let him sleep there. Said it's the least they can do."

I put my hand to my heart. That was so nice. Humans can be so nice.

Johnson tapped the roof of the car and opened the back, then bent to look in on me. "Okay?"

I was leaning against the door, my legs bent, one on the seat and the other resting on the floor. My skirt had slid up my thighs. "I believe you were saying that it's your sworn duty to protect and serve? I could use a little servicing right about now, officer."

He looked between my legs and grinned broadly. He brought his gaze up and the grin held, then slid away. His focus was on the window behind my head and not on me. He stood up, and I swiveled around to see what was happening.

Holy moly! Unicorns!

CHAPTER TWO

"WHAT?" Kay stopped dead in her tracks on the sidewalk. She gripped my arm to stop me, too.

I threw back my head and laughed. "I kid you not. Unicorns. People dressed up in these getups that looked like colorful horses, but with horns." I drew my hand out from my forehead to as far as it could reach to show her how they looked. "Sparkly, too."

"And they had tails?"

I could see the confusion on her face. "Beautiful long flowing tails that blew in the wind. I didn't think about it in the moment, but now that I look back on it, imagine the strength it would take to hold those tails in place. That's darned impressive."

"You mean they were...just kind of stuck in...place?"

"Looked that way to me."

"Huh, talk about a tight ass."

I snorted.

"What did you do? Did you go down and see what was going on?"

"Well Johnson felt responsible for my safety. He also had to investigate what the heck they were doing. So he drove me home, and then went back to see what was up. He said he'd fill me in later."

"I bet he wanted to fill you in later." She bumped into me. "Nothing like a little unicorn boffing to put a guy in the mood."

"Well, while that kind of filling in is entirely welcome, it's not what I meant. I want to know what the heck was happening down there but I haven't heard from him."

"Connor said it was a busy night at the station. Full moon brings out the loonies."

Connor Fitzgerald was Kay's brother, and the two of them were my dearest friends. He was a sergeant with the police force, and while he was smart, cute, and wore the blue uniform with the shiny badge that made my engines purr, he was off-limits.

I loved him too much to play with him.

Besides, he had a different sexual ethic than I did. He only liked his sex to be driven by a relationship. And I most decidedly did not.

I actually kind of have an undiagnosed allergy to romantic relationships. To each his own, as I liked to say.

"Still, I'd really like to hear the whole kinky story," I said.

"Hey," Kay said, "Do you know the difference between kinky and perverted?"

"No what?"

"Kinky, they use a feather and perverted the use the whole damned duck."

"That's quackers."

We started down the street again, my Rottweiler, Twinkles, sniffing along the route.

"I wonder why Peter hasn't gotten in touch yet. Usually if you leave a guy hanging, he's sprinting to get back in the race." I scowled.

Kay flicked a finger toward Silberstein's Deli.

I nodded agreement with her choice for lunch. "Oh, he wasn't hanging when I left him. He was still in the ready, set, go position, poor guy." I gave Kay a broad wink. "Duty first. I texted him but I haven't heard back yet. He didn't get off until three. He probably hit the showers, then hit the hay. But you're right. He didn't finish hitting on me, so he'll be calling soon."

"Poor boy, all that coitus interruptus. I hate that!"

"Poor boy? Poor me! Damned unicorns," I grumbled, which made Kay laugh.

We stopped outside the storefront, and I sat on the bench to wait since I had Twinkles with us and dogs, especially 130-pound Rottweilers, weren't welcome inside. "The usual, please," I called as Kay went in.

As I turned my face to the sun to get my daily dose of bone-strengthening vitamin D (as my dad liked to say), I thought about Marley and wondered what he was eating today. I opened the door and poked my head in. "Hey, Kay, how about you double my order, and we go up and see if Marley wouldn't like to join us for a picnic."

"And a chat?"

I shrugged. "Might as well hear the story straight from the horse's mouth."

Kay tipped her head back and forth as if she were considering. "Yeah, a horse will work if you can't get it straight from the unicorn. There are some family ties, I'm assuming," she said.

KAY HELD the handle on our food bag, I held the lead for Twinkles, and off we went, headed for the graveyard. I am, in general, not a fan of graveyards. But it was such a beautiful day, I was enjoying the walk.

My whole life was pretty much lived in a stamp-sized portion of our fair city of Jamesburg, Virginia.

The bar I managed and hoped to co-own one day, called Hooch's, was three blocks from my apartment and three blocks from Kay's place, though that trail was a bit of a zigzag. The police station sat one block east of the bar.

The area had great places to eat dotted all over. Plenty of parks, shops, and coffeehouses. Most of my friends lived right down in this area in lofts that were made when the tobacco warehouses were converted into millennial housing.

Everything was in walking distance. The only reason I had a car was for ease of grocery shopping, wimpiness when it came to inclement weather, and, of course, visiting my dad.

"So where exactly does this Marley guy live?" Kay asked after we had walked several blocks. We could see the tall stone walls that surrounded the grounds and held the remains of some of the first families to live in Virginia.

"A mausoleum somewhere."

She stopped with a look of incredulity. "You mean you don't know?"

"Kay," I sighed. "I was hiding from the homeless guy on the floor of Johnson's cruiser, trying to get my panties back in place. I wasn't asking Johnson to draw me a map. At that point, I thought we were done dealing with the interruption and were going to get back to business."

"Monkey business." Kay swung her hip to bump me, and chuckled. We made our way to the wrought iron arch that read St. Clemmons'.

Kay looked around and sighed. "I wish there was a directory somewhere."

"Yup, we could look up the homeless Vietnam vet and go over and ring his bell."

"Funny." She shot me a dry look that told me my sarcasm wasn't helpful. "I only have an hour lunch break and I used most of it walking."

"When do you need to be back?"

"Mrph, don't know. They owe me a bunch of overtime hours back, so I guess I'm not all that worried about it. Besides, I changed all the passwords in the computers and files. If they fire me, I'm not likely to be able to recall what they were."

"Smart."

She nodded. "Job security. Single girl's got to do what a single girl's got to do."

"Single, huh? Have you heard from Terrence?"

"I did. He's flying back from London to hang out with me this weekend. So looks like our off-again/on-again relationship switch has been flipped back to on."

"Good news." And I meant it. Kay was happiest when she was with Terrence.

And Terrence, while he was a jet-setting Internet star, understood that the girls flinging themselves at him were flashes in the pan. They didn't really know him and love him the way his oldest friends and family did.

Certainly not the way Kay did. I was both proud of him and wished him well, but also wished his starlight would dim, and he could come back home. Angel. Devil.

We set off down the first path on the right. I called out tentatively, "Mr. Marley, sir?" every once in a while.

Twinkles's nose went up in the air. His head was like an oscillating fan, sucking in air, processing it through, making sure that everything in a hundred-and-fifty-degree arc was covered.

Boom.

It was like a fighter pilot—"Tango has been targeted. I have a lock. Firing." Zoom. He jetted out of my hand and tore over the grass. Past the sign that specifically said, "Stay off the grass." Too bad Twinkles couldn't read.

Whether I wanted to or not—and I most decidedly did not—I chased over the tops of folks's graves after my dog. Up on my tip-toes, flailing my arms and begging for forgiveness. "Sorry. Sorry! Please, don't haunt me."

When I caught him, Twinkles was licking something off the ground.

My heart stopped. Did someone put something out here to poison the stray animals and wildlife?

I pushed Twinkles to the side, which only worked because he was focused, and I surprised him. He wasn't braced.

There was a pile of poop. Weird-looking poop. Twinkles gave me a push that landed me on my butt. Because I was focused, and he surprised me. I wasn't braced. It took me a second to figure out what I was seeing.

The poop was covered in pastel colored mini marshmallows in the shapes of stars, moons, and rainbows, and crafting glitter. Lots of glitter.

Twinkles dove in, his eyes rolled up and fixed on me, his tongue greedily lapping up the high fructose corn syrup.

I knew it was a lost cause trying to stop him, so I pulled out my phone and did a quick Google search for marshmallow toxicity and dogs.

Kay ran up beside us. Holding a stitch in her side, she dropped our lunch on the grass. "I didn't dress for jogging," she gasped, plopping down beside me and resting against a tombstone that read, "Adam Spanks, His Beloved Wife Marybelle".

Kay looked smart in her business attire – except for those pantyhose with white sport socks and sneakers. And now, I'm assuming, grass stains on her fanny.

Kay glanced over. "What the hell is he eating?"

"Licking. I'm pretty sure that's unicorn poop."

When Twinkles had finally eaten the last marshmallow –which, by the way, was listed as not toxic to dogs but still not a good idea; ditto with the glitter—he allowed us to move on. I continued to call for Marley.

As we headed down another path, a woman was moving our way. Her eyes scanned over the ground, searching for something.

Kay elbowed me. "Is that Felicia Mulvane?"

I squinted and pushed my head forward, trying to get a better look. "Could be. Wonder what she lost."

Felicia was moving at a snail's pace, but we were moving at a Twinkles's pace, so we were soon close enough to call to her. Kay had known her better than I did since they had been on the same soccer team, so Kay did the honors.

Up shot Kay's hand, and she gave it a wave. "Felicia? Felicia, is that you?"

The woman's head came up, a smile crossed over her face, she turned and took one last glance behind her, then headed over our way.

"Did you lose something? Can we help?"

"What?" Felicia asked, her face turning pink. "Oh, no. No. Thank you. I was out here looking for four-leaf clovers. And," she hefted out a sigh and a shrug, "I haven't found a single one." Felicia brushed her dirty blonde hair out of her face as the wind picked up a notch and blew a strand under her nose.

Twinkles's nose went back in the air. I shook a finger at him and said, "Oh no you don't."

He ignored me completely. It wasn't Twinkles's fault. He'd been ejected from his puppy good behavior class on the very first night. His sheer size had freaked out humans and fellow class pups alike. But hey, we made a bonus twenty bucks if we promised never to come back.

Kay grabbed Felicia's hand. "Oh my goodness!" Kay stared down at the ice cube sitting on Felicia's left ring finger. "You're engaged. Congratulations. That's awesome," Kay said as she pulled her high school friend into a hug. "Why are you looking for four-leaf clovers if you snagged a guy who can get you such a beautiful ring?"

It was beautiful, if you liked audaciously ginormous diamonds on your finger. It was a little gaudy for my taste.

"It is beautiful, isn't it?" She held up her hand to let the sun sparkle on it. She and Kay admired it together, then Felicia dropped her hand. "Yeah, but my job just got axed with the new budget."

"Won't your fiancé help out?" Kay asked just as Twinkles took off, finally having homed in on the new scent he wanted to investigate. And I took off after him. God forbid he think it was a good idea to try to dig up a bone out here. I mean, seriously.

Two rows over he'd found another pile of unicorn poo and was happily licking it like a kid who got his first ice cream of summer.

I waited with a tapping toe.

He shuffled over so I could hold his lead and walk back to Kay. The lead was a sham. It lead gave me zero control.

The only thing this lead did was keep me from getting a citation for not having one, and that's it.

Kay looked up.

"Unicorn poo."

Kay stuck out her tongue. "He's going to get so sick," she said as I reinserted myself back into the conversation.

"I'm strong and capable and all that," Felicia was saying. "I just need to find a good job, or even a half-assed job until a good one comes along."

"A half-assed job?" I said. "I have one of those open." I brightened at the prospect of being able to help.

Felicia tilted her head.

"Have you heard of Hooch's Bar? I'm the manager there."

"It's next to Nicky's?"

I sucked in some air. To use Nicky's as a landmark around me was just plain rude. That man was trying to run me out of business. Which, of course, would mean I'd be in Felicia's position of looking for a new job – a job that might just require corporate dress with panty hose. And wearing panty hose was a prison sentence.

Felicia sent a questioning look to Kay. Kay gave her a subtle shake of the head that said about as clearly as possible, "Drop it."

"It's a block from the police department?" Felicia sent a quick glance to Kay to make sure that was a safer geographical location to mention. She got the nod.

"That's right," I said. "I'm looking for someone full-time. You get ten an hour plus tips. After the probation period, you get health insurance. Seven to two, Tuesday to Saturday. Sunday and Mondays, we're closed."

"Seven pm until two am?"

"Yeah, in general bars don't get a lot of patronage at

seven in the morning." My snarky little comment slipped out. Mrph. I could be such a wiseass. And that didn't bode well when I was trying to make a new hire.

I really needed someone, too.

I was new to running the bar by myself. Hooch had taken off for an extended leave of absence, and Kay had been working two jobs to help me out for the last couple of weeks.

I couldn't let that happen much longer – it was too much for her.

Felicia reached out to hold my arm. "That actually works out really well. It would leave me time to search for a job during normal working hours, and I can make my bills." She paused, looking at her feet, considering. "I can see Stewart during the day." She looked up. "Yes, I think I'd like to work for you. Of course, you know I'm hoping it's really temporary."

"Understood," I said.

Kay tapped me. "I have to get back. I'm going to eat my lunch at my desk."

"Okay, good, I'll walk with you." I turned to Felicia. "So glad we ran into you. Be at the bar tonight at seven, and we'll get you started. Casual attire, comfortable shoes with rubber soles."

"Gotcha."

I was disappointed that I hadn't been able to leave the food for Marley. He had touched a chord for me. Yeah, though I have to admit only part of it was kindheartedness– some of it was just plain out curiosity. I wanted the story behind the unicorn poo.

We rounded out of the gate.

"Didn't you say that the unicorns danced under the full moon for three days?" Kay asked.

"Yup." I turned and shielded my eyes so I could scan one last time for Marley.

"Which day do you think last night was? The first day of the full moon?"

I pulled out my phone and touched my elbow to Kay's arm so she could steer me while I did a Google search. "Today is the official full moon, so I'd say yesterday was day one. Why?"

"I was just thinking about what we were saying back at the deli. It's okay to get it from the horse's mouth but wouldn't it be more accurate to get it from the unicorn's? If they come out at midnight. How long do you think they hang out? A couple of hours, maybe?"

I stopped. "What are you thinking?"

"That it might be fun to go on a wild unicorn safari. And I'm pretty sure I know where Connor keeps his field glasses. Game?"

A grin spread across my face. "Holy shit. Yes!"

CHAPTER THREE

THE VERY FIRST thing I remember when I was a baby—and I mean baby, baby still in a diaper—was the concept of memory.

My dad was driving into the driveway, and I ran toward him full of a story about something that had happened that morning.

It was memorable in that it was shocking. Not the thing that happened that morning—which was probably that I saw a bug or something equally momentous in a toddler's eyes—no, the reason I remember it was that my little baby brain was blown!

Until that moment, I hadn't processed the idea of the whole "past tense" thing. It was my first glimmer of an understanding about the time/space continuum.

I didn't have the words to say, "earlier today." So, I buried that story and didn't tell it to him.

Instead, I pulled off my diaper in the sandbox and played kitty cat.

Yeah, I was *that* kind of kid. The whole "why not" thing

and the whole "might as well give it a try" thing are how I've navigated through life from the very first point I can remember until now.

The second important memory I have came a little later. I had graduated to big-girl panties and was enrolled at the Children's Garden Preschool.

I was about two and a half, and as an only child with a dad who was gone twenty-four hours at a time as a fireman and a mom who was busy entertaining "Uncle Clem," I was used to keeping myself company.

The first time I walked into a room full of kids my age sent my system into shock. I think it was the same feeling someone on an acid trip might have. There was way too much movement and color and noise to spring on a girl all at once. (And probably the reason I don't do drugs today.)

Our teacher herded us together and told us to sit down in a circle, crisscross applesauce. To me that was a bunch of nonsense words, so I stood watching as kids plopped to the ground.

A pretty little girl with long red hair and a buttercup-colored dress reached out and took my hand. "I'm going to be your best friend," she said. It was a fact. A done deal. I believed her then, and I believe it now.

Mary Katherine Fitzgerald, Kay, was my first friend, my best friend, my lifelong friend.

Kay moved over and put her hand on my shoulder. "You're looking nostalgic."

"Mmm, contemplative is more like it. I'm trying to decide what to do with this wall." We were standing in the middle of the main room at Hooch's.

Felicia slogged over to stand next to us. She was wearing slim jeans, a peek-a-boo blouse and rain boots. It was the only thing she could find with rubber soles. She said she'd go shopping for a different pair of shoes in the morning.

"I think your boots are cute," Kay said. "You might be able to find a pair of rubber soled cowboy boots. That would be great with your outfit."

"Hey Kay, speaking of cowboy boots, do you know why I prefer cops to cowboys?"

"No, why?"

"Because cops know a good ride lasts longer than five seconds."

Kay clutched my arm, and bent over snort-giggling.

Felicia wrinkled her nose, then redirected our attention to the wall. "Why?" she asked. "What needs to be done to the wall? It's beautiful."

She was right—it was absolutely stunning, I thought as I pursed my lips and dragged them to the side, considering it.

The wall was decorated with a large mural of a German shepherd done in modern multi-colored tones. Fido had a thick police collar around his neck, and he sported a badge.

I wanted to attract the police crowd to my bar. They drank a lot, which made my cash register happy. Besides, they had interesting stories to tell when they'd been tipping back a bottle or six. Not the normal drunken she-broke-my-heart stories. I mean really good stories, the kind that make you cringe and chuckle at the same time. Like *I was trying to get my game on in the back seat of my car when I was interrupted by a homeless vet who needed me to stop a war between the unicorns and the Death Eaters.* Ah, humanity.

The dog, I thought, was a great idea. It really added to the "police are welcome and honored here" atmosphere. But the dog had been painted by a guy who had tried to sweep Kay off her feet. She wanted to be swept, too. And then things went to hell in a handbasket. This is a prime example of why I have an allergic reaction to relationships.

I glanced over at her. "The dog has to go," I said.

Twinkles whined.

"Not you, baby," I reached down and scratched behind his ears. "I'll get some paint and do it tomorrow."

"Leave the painting," Kay said, pulling the elastic from her hair and fluffing her strawberry blonde curls. She put the elastic on her wrist. "I like it."

I put my hands on my hips, a sign that I was willing to rumble. "No. It needs to go." I pointed a sweeping finger to show the expanse of the wall. "I was thinking about painting it police uniform blue. Then I can paint the wall behind the bar white to keep things from getting too dim. You need to help me figure out what to put on the wall." I snapped my fingers and pointed. "Twinkles, go to my office."

Twinkles dragged himself up and walked through the door. I listened as he plopped back down.

Kay had her arms crossed over her chest now. I bet she realized I was using Twinkles to distract her from the subject. "I'm serious," she said. "Leave the mural be. If you paint over it, I'll assume you're calling me weak."

I knew that tone in her voice. The same tone she used when we she announced we'd be best friends twenty years ago. It was her "here is the law, don't fuck with me" tone. Yup–she used it at age two. A force to be reckoned with, when she was in this mood. That tone was rarely worth the fight. I'd have to leave the dog.

I moved behind the bar and got a fat Sharpie I used to make signs. I skittered over to the wall and plopped down beside the signature of He Who Must Not Be Named.

"Fido gives us street cred with the badges," Kay said.

"Agreed." I pulled the cap off with my teeth and spit it into my lap.

"Now what are you doing?" Felicia asked.

"Every dog needs a bone." I stuck my tongue out the corner of my mouth like I did when I applied mascara and needed to concentrate, drew an outline around the signature, and started to color it in.

I looked up from my masterpiece when the bar door jingled. Connor, dressed in a sharply pressed uniform and his shiny badge, was making his way in. Oh, and look, Ashley was in tow. I rolled my eyes and went back to my work.

"What're you doing, Bobbi Jax?" Connor asked.

Few people call me Bobbi Jax. They'd have to have known me for a long time. When I started high school, I wanted to be called BJ. I thought it was edgy. Now I just thought it was funny.

Connor and Kay never made the switch – none of my family did. And family was made in the heart, not in DNA, right? Right. That was why Connor still called me Bobbi Jax and the bitch on his arm called me BJ. Mrph – shouldn't think thoughts like that. They might just slip out at inopportune moments. Like when she was within earshot.

"I'm giving the dog a bone," I said.

Connor squinted. "Looks more like a boner from this angle."

I tried to line my visual field up with his. Yup, he was right. Well, I *had* been thinking about Johnson. I grinned. "I'm not done yet. Stop judging."

Felicia came out of the back room and looked over our way.

"Oh, look, Fellatio's here." Ashley looked like she'd licked a lemon.

"Hey there, RBF." Felicia set the rack of steins on the counter and began putting them away.

"RBF?" Kay asked. (Thank you, Kay!)

"Resting Bitch Face. It's what everyone I knew in high school called her."

Ashley swung her head and gave Connor the oh-no-she-didn't duck face, letting him know he should come to her defense.

Instead, he lifted his hand. "I'm on duty. I was meeting Ashley for dinner and now I need to head back in. I just stopped by to tell you, Kay, that Mom says you're to come to mass on Sunday and back to the house afterwards. She wants your help making wedding shower plans for Pam."

"You mean she wants me to come over so she can guilt me for not having my own fiancé."

"Probably." He sent her a lopsided smile that read as *better you than me*. "She is a Catholic mother. She'd be derelict in her duties if she wasn't guilting you about something. Take Bobbi Jax." He lifted his chin toward me. "She can be your wingman."

Kay looked at me.

"Who's Pam?" I asked.

"Younger cousin."

"Ah. Free food? I'm all over it." I waved to Connor as he left with Ashley stomping out behind him.

The three of us stared at the door after it banged shut.

There was a group release of stressed air from our lungs.

I caught Kay's eye. "I thought Terrance was going to be in town."

"He is, darn it," Kay said. She turned to Felicia. "Let's change the subject. Why don't you tell us about your fiancé? What does he do for a living?"

"Jeweler." She smiled. "Stewart Gottlieb. He owns Gottlieb's Jewelers."

"You mean the jewelers on the other side of Main Street? The family that folks nicknamed 'Got Rocks?'"

"Yes, that's him." Felicia grinned.

Kay slid onto a stool and posted her elbows on the counter, hunkering down for some good old-fashioned girl gossip. "I hear their ads on the radio all the time. They say they've been a family-run business for a hundred and fifty years."

"Yup, and Stewart needs an heir to carry it on." She rubbed a hand over her belly.

"He's an only child?"

"He has a half-brother who doesn't care a fig about carat weight and stone clarity. He thinks that's a sissy business for men who were born without testosterone. Frank Mason. He does construction. Or as he calls it, 'a real man's job.'"

"Mason?"

"Illegitimate brother, only claimed by Stewart Bartholomew Gottlieb IV after his wife's death. Frank got included in his daddy's will, which, of course, is very upsetting. I suggested they run DNA tests and everything." She shrugged. "Science says that Frank is, in fact, his daddy's son."

I moved around to sit on a stool next to Kay's, wishing for a bowl of popcorn. "Dun dah dun!"

"Are the brothers about the same age?" Kay asked.

"Oh no, not even close." Felicia shook her head. "Frank is my age."

Kay and I shot looks at each other, then turned our heads in unison back to Felicia. "Gottlieb sounds like he must be pretty old," I said.

Kay swatted me.

I cleared my throat. "Do you mind my asking how old he is?" I asked.

Felicia reached for a glass. "Ninety-six this year," she said. The sound of her pouring herself a diet soda only partially covered up the gasp of air that Kay and I sucked in.

Felicia wrinkled her brow.

Kay wriggled around on her stool looking uncomfortable. "Don't you think that's a little bit of an age difference for a married couple?" she asked.

"What?" Felicia asked, obviously very confused by our wide-eyed looks of shock.

"Well, you're what? Twenty-threeish, so he's sixty-some odd years older than you," Kay said. "That's kinda taking May-December to an extreme."

"No. Oh, no." She put her hand on her chest and laughed. My soon-to-be father-in-law is ninety-six. That would be a terrible age difference." She gave a full-body shiver. "Ew. No." She laughed. "My Stewart, Stewart Bartholomew Gottlieb V, is only fifty-eight. Stewart IV had Frank when he was seventy. If my Stewart's like his daddy, we have plenty of time to have an heir and maybe even a spare." She winked.

Kay and I wrinkled our noses. Fifty-eight. That was my dad's age. Ew! I think I might have vomited a little in my mouth.

Felicia looked over at the door, then back around to me. "Is it always this dead?"

We didn't have a single patron. Mrph. "It's Tuesday, the slowest day of the week. But yeah. This is way too dead to be good." We'd had a dozen or so people stop by earlier in the evening, but none of them settled in. Most of them just needed a jolt of goodwill to get them through the night and moved on. "I need another marketing idea. One that will help me steal—I mean earn—the loyalty of the cops away from Dollars to Doughnuts, the pub up the street."

"Maybe you need a name change?" Felicia asked.

"From Hooch's? Nah. Our name may not have doughnuts in it, but our signature scotch is Badge Bunny Booze," I explained.

Felicia drew her brow together. "Is that something officers like?"

"Scotch or badge bunnies?" Kay leaned her weight onto the counter. "I'd say yes in both cases."

"That's a thing? Badge bunnies? What's it mean?" Felicia reached down to shove her pants leg back into her rain boot.

"It's someone who finds cops to be as sexy as hell and acts on it," I said with a smile.

"Huh," Felicia said, turning to scowl at Fido, the German shepherd adorning the wall. I couldn't tell whether she was thinking about badge bunnies or contemplating the art. I let her be as I straightened up the counter space. God forbid another ABC inspector shows up and finds a lemon out of place.

"I think that would work," Felicia said, tapping a finger on her chin.

"What's that?" I asked as I gathered the top of the trash and knotted it.

"Why not get some hot buff officers to pose for photographs with puppies from the shelter? Turn it into a calendar. Sell it around with your logo on it. The proceeds could go to buying a police service dog, or whatever they need. Training, maybe. And we could put information about the shelter dogs and how to adopt a pet and stuff like that on each month's page. Then you can have a series of events where the cops were here, maybe a few at a time, get it out on social media. Buff handsome do-gooder guys pull in girls, girls pull in other guys, soon the place is swarming"

"It's May," Kay pointed out. "No one's buying a calendar until at least October."

Felicia held up a finger. "Unless of course you made it an eighteen-month calendar. More puppies. More hunky heroes. More hunky hero events. Say three guys per event—that would last six Saturdays. 'Come and meet Officer September, Officer July, and Officer May and cuddle with the puppies!' That would attract the girls, don't you think?" Felicia looked over at me.

"Kind of an unfair thing to ask that of Bobbi Jax," Kay said with a grin. "For her it's an emphatic yes. But you're right. It would bring in girls who like cops and puppies. And cops—who we want to hang out here—would like to meet the kinds of girls who would find them desirable."

"Connor would do that for you, wouldn't he? Pose for a picture with a puppy, I mean." Felicia shot a look toward me with a raised brow. "A picture of him would sell a ton of calendars, I'd think. And maybe Connor would know who else to ask."

Kay snorted. "Yeah, I think it might be more Bobbi Jax here who might know. My brother's not big into scoping out hunky cops."

"I think it's a really good idea, Felicia," I said. "I'll start thinking of cops who might be willing to do a good turn."

NOT LONG AFTER, I sent Felicia home. I wasn't making enough money to cover her salary, and to be honest, the squelching noise her rain boots was making was driving me up the damned wall. I moved over and flipped the sign to read "Closed" and locked the door behind Felicia.

Okay. If I was going to be really honest, I wanted to get the bar cleaned up and shut down early. It was coming up on midnight and no one had been in for the last half hour. I doubted anyone would come in for the rest of the night. I turned to lift a chair onto a table to clear the floor for a sweep and a mop.

"I see we're getting ready to go on safari." Kay hefted up a bar stool and set it on the counter.

"Smart girl. Did you get the binoculars?"

"Two pairs. I also got us a bag of black clothes."

I hooked my arm around Kay's neck and hugged her tight as we both busted up laughing.

CHAPTER FOUR

KAY and I were dressed from head to toe in black, creeping down the sidewalk in unicorn voyeur stealth mode. We'd pulled hoodies over our hair and cranked down on the ties so our faces peeked out of the pucker of fabric.

"You look like an asshole," Kay whispered.

"Thanks, you, too." I tapped her shoulder strap. "What have you got in the backpack."

"I borrowed dad's binoculars instead of Connor's. Connor's glasses are tactical, but Dad has the sportsmen's kind. The ones he uses for birding had a built in digital camera. The other he uses for hunting, and it had night vision so he could make his way out in the woods before the crack of dawn—which has some kind of caveman appeal to him that I can't fathom."

"So we can tape unicorn porn?"

"Yuppers," she said.

"What if they see us doing that?"

"I brought a couple bags of glitter to toss in their direction. I thought maybe it might work like catnip, and they'd fall into a unicorn nirvana. Stop drop and roll in the sparkle of it all, and they'd forget all about us."

"Sounds like a good plan."

We debated Twinkles as a teammate. Cons–he could be darned loud. He went where he wanted, when he wanted. He liked to eat unicorn poo. Pros–he also liked to eat bad guys.

"Pros win!" Kay called, the decision made.

It didn't take us far down the road to rethink that decision. A few blocks, as a matter of fact.

Twinkles pulled his lead free from Kay's hand and raced toward a patch of primo grass that he wanted to water. Then BOOM, he switched gears and raced off in another direction. He galloped down an alley that seemed to vacuum up light like a black hole sucks up stars.

"Crap," I said.

Twinkles howled.

"Double crap," Kay said. "Go get him." She pushed me forward.

I slapped her away and pushed her forward, "You go get him. You're the one who said pros win."

"Twinkle Bell," she called, patting her thighs. "Twinkle Bell come her to Auntie Kay. Look, here's some yummy unicorn poop!"

I smacked at her. "Don't say that, you're elevating poop into a delicacy."

It was just after midnight. I didn't think twice about a stroll to the cemetery. After all, we were walking in the protective halo of the police department that was only a couple of blocks away. Few people were stupid enough to look for trouble in this neighborhood. But someone or some*thing* was down that alley with my dog. I could hear the moans.

"What is that sound," I asked.

"Wind?" Kay offered.

I licked my finger and stuck it in the air. "Meh."

"It's a ghost. Moaning Myrtle." She clapped her hands. "Come on, Twinkles let's go."

"You mean Luna Looooooovegood."

She pushed her hoodie down and tilted her ear toward the sound. "That doesn't sound like schtupping to me. I think someone's in trouble."

"Trouble-trouble or homeless guy crouching behind the trash bin with gastrointestinal issues trouble?"

We stared into the void.

Was this 911 worthy? I mean, I wasn't actually shy about calling cops.

It might even be fun to see who might show up. But I also didn't want to piss them off if they were busy taking care of something important.

There it was again that horrible moan met by Twinkles high-pitched whine. I took a step forward. "I can't imagine what's making that sound." No. That wasn't true. I could imagine. I had a whole lot of imaginings going on and all the pictures that I was conjuring had to do with nineteen-eighties horror flicks and the stupidity of the teens going to check out the banging noise in the basement.

Bang.

See? It was a set up. But Twinkles was down there. He wasn't coming out, and I was his mama. Even though I was twenty-two, I was going to be that teen. Crappity crap crap. "I'm coming buddy," I called and took another step forward.

Kay gripped at my arm. She knew what I'd do next. And she obviously thought it was a bad choice. This was our relationship in a nutshell. Her pragmatism helped to weigh down my ballooning impulsivity. She was my anchor

– well, anchor might be pushing it. At least she stopped me long enough that I remembered to hatchet-shake my phone's flashlight on.

Holding my phone's light out in front of me, I took another step forward, shaking my arm to divest myself of Kay's tight grip.

I'd read in a police novel that there was a cone of safety behind a light. That the person who was looking in that direction would see light but not what was behind it. That way, if they were shooting a gun or running forward with a knife, they wouldn't have a good target.

Hmm.

Maybe holding the light directly in front of me was a bad idea. I didn't know for sure if someone was down the alley. If there was, the chance of them having a weapon was probably slim to none. *But* if they shot at the light, I definitely wanted it to miss me. I stretched my arm out the side.

Twinkles was howling now. I'd never heard him make noises like that before. He was a hundred and thirty-pound Rottweiler and growling was his usual take on new situations.

Not this time.

Twinkles noises set my nerves on fire.

Kay was beside me. "Don't go down there after him, Bobbi Jax. Just don't."

"Well someone has to. Did you want to take lead?"

I looked at her. She looked at me we both stuck out a fist. "Rock. Paper. Scissors. Shoot," we sang. We both stuck out scissor hands. Everyone knows you always go for scissors first.

"Together then," she said.

We gripped hands like Daphne and Velma creeping up on the monster in the abyss

Kay pulled out her phone. "We need a Fred," she said. "And some Scooby snacks."

I took another step forward while Kay yelled into the phone challenging Connor to get here now – lights and sirens. Her hand never left my back. We were headed in together. That's what we did. For better or for worse, for stupid or for... "Shit, what *is* that?"

Twinkles was up against the pile, pushing it with his nose. The pile moved, and I nearly jumped out of my skin. Kay let out a shrill scream, then pulled her phone back out of her pocket. Scrolling. Tapping.

The pile moaned.

Kay was talking to someone, but my focus was on making my feet move forward. Twinkles would warn me if this was dangerous, right?

I cast my light up and down the bundle and let my mind process. Finally, I realized it was a woman, her eyes wide, face almost hidden by a wool cap. She seemed to be hidden somewhere under the volume of clothes she was wearing.

My first thought was that she was overcome by heat. It was a lovely mid-sixties evening, the perfect temperature if you're not cocooned in so much fleece.

Twinkles had inched closer until he lay side by side with her. Nudging her. Encouraging her.

She had one hand on Twinkles, the other clutched at her chest.

I scrambled forward. Okay...okay... I needed to do something. I just had to land on the right thing. Hooch made me keep my first aid and CPR certifications up to date. I had skills. Mostly bandaging paper cut skills. But something. The first step was to ask permission. The next was to pull on gloves. I had no gloves. "Ma'am? I'm BJ. Is it okay if I help?"

Her response could have been a nod of assent or could have been her gasp for air. I was taking it as a yes. ABC – Airway? Check. Breath? Kinda. Circulation? Since her eyes were open and blinking, I knew she had a pulse.

I straddled the woman and gripped her outer coat. Twisting, I dragged her around until I got the woman into a straight line and not the odd spiral she had landed in. My hands fell away from their grip on her lapels.

Her eyes rolled back in her head and her tongue lolled to the side. "Hey I've seen this before, she's drunk."

"She's not drunk," Kay said. "She's passed out."

"Passed out drunk," I said.

Kay waved her hand over the woman's mouth. "She's not breathing," she said. "She needs CPR."

"Okay, I'll do compressions, You do the breaths."

"How 'bout I do the compressions and you do the breaths?"

We both stuck our fists out "Rock. Paper. Scissors. Shoot."

Kay stuck out rock. I stuck out paper. I stabbed a victorious fist in the air and pushed Twinkles out of the way so I could hunker down beside her. She was dressed like a babushka in a Siberian blizzard.

I got three jackets unfastened before I found her sweater layers. Nothing I could do about it. I gave it my best guess on where to put my hands, and with locked elbows, I started the compressions, fast and hard, fueled with a spike of adrenaline.

I was sweating big-time. This was exhausting work. I couldn't have been compressing as long as I felt I had. It felt like hours.

"Kay, we have to switch next breath. You need to get ready. I need a break," I gasped out.

Kay and I were okay on the fitness scale. I mean, we hit the gym with some regularity, but that was more to save money on buying new clothes when we'd overindulged on the carbs than an actual dedication to our good health and efficacy with our CPR skills.

Twinkles scrambled onto all fours and circled around me at a sprint, taking off up the alley. I could hear his barking. This time it sounded like a signal—help must have arrived.

"Twenty-eight, twenty-nine, thirty. Switch." Help being here, somewhere on the street, still wasn't help being *here,* taking over the work. Twinkles pointing the way would mean they'd find us faster.

Time did a weird little hiccup.

Connor was hunkering by Kay's side. "On three, switch." He took over. He compressed the lady's chest twice.

Boom!

Her eyes popped open.

The homeless woman and I were staring eyeball to eyeball. My lids were stretched wide in surprise. Her eyelids were stretched wide in confusion. I mean it's not every day you wake up with a stranger pinching you nose. And I'm sure the seal I had made around her mouth was shocking too.

Well, she shocked the *shit* out of me; that's for sure.

I immediately rocked back on my heels. That had to be ranked up with one of the odder moments in my life–and my life was well-fertilized with odd moments.

Dad appeared at my side. He pulled me to my feet and pointed us out of the way of the rescue team. Then I went to join Connor and Kay out by the street.

Twinkles sat beside Connor, acting like a good boy and

not the kind of boy who runs down dark alleys, though, thank God, he did.

"What were you thinking, Bobbi Jax?" Connor asked. His brow was scrunched into a furrow that I almost never saw there.

I understood why he was scowling at me. He cared. "I was thinking that Twinkles's stomach was making weird squeaking noises." I reached for my dog's lead. "He needed to find a patch of grass to find some relief, then he jerked away from me and played Lassie saving that poor woman."

"You call 911 and you wait." Cop voice, full-tilt.

"If I'd waited she'd be dead." I held back on the foot-stomping. There must be an age where that became too juvenile to help you make your point, and I was pretty sure I'd blown out those birthday candles already.

Connor lifted his chin. I was right.

"You would have run in. That's what good people do." My voice was challenging. I wanted him to say we'd done the right thing.

"I have a sworn duty. And training."

I canted my head. "And I'm a human being."

Again, that little lift of his chin that said *you win.* I guessed body language was as good as English language in some circumstances. I understood this was the best he could do. He didn't like it when he thought Kay or I were in danger.

Twinkles's stomach made a weird squelching sound like Felicia in her rubber rain boots, and he pulled at his lead. I had it wrapped around my wrist. Only one escape per night, and he'd hit that quota. The three of us strolled after him. It was quite the shift in energy from the scrambling rescue crews working behind us. I was glad to walk away.

And to be perfectly honest, I wanted to wash my face and gargle with some whisky.

Twinkles, though, was taking his sweet time. He was a connoisseur pottier. He sniffs and ambles to the best possible location to leave his mark and declare that he is king of this jungle. We moved down the road as he continued his hunt.

"Far enough," Connor said. "Let's turn him around."

I gave the lead a tug.

Did I mention Twinkles was a hundred thirty pounds of muscle? Did I mention he only humored us with compliance when he wanted to? When Twinkles was on a task, mere mortals had no power. He'd stretched the lead out as far as my arm could reach. I jogged up a few feet. "Twinkles, stop pulling." Fortunately, it looked like he'd found the place to make his mark – a small patch of grass near the street light.

"Have a plastic bag?" That was Connor being a cop—law and order, no poop left behind.

I pulled one from my pocket and waved it around.

Twinkles squatted down, took a few hovering steps and left a pile of poop, like soft-serve pistachio ice cream bedazzled in sparkles.

The three of us looked down.

"Well," Connor said, "isn't that fancy?"

CHAPTER FIVE

WE RECONVENED AT THE BAR. Kay and I had quickly changed back into our normal clothes, hoping no one would ask about our earlier black attire. I just wasn't in the mood to explain that we'd been heading out on a unicorn safari.

Boo, we missed the unicorns.

As if reading my mind, Kay leaned in and whispered in my ear. "According to Marley, we still have one more shot at this tomorrow night. And if we miss that? We always have the next full moon."

I sent her a smile. I loved that about her. Never deterred.

Connor was playing host, standing behind the bar, setting out the shot glasses, and pouring the Irish whisky, a time-honored punctuation mark to an end of our adventures.

Connor got a phone call as he pushed the shot glasses our way. We waited for him while he looked at the screen and wrinkled his nose like someone had stepped in shit and was tracking it in. It had to be Ashley who left a text. Why did he stick with her? It had been eight long years now. Ever since he was a junior in high school. It wasn't like their relationship was going anywhere. They avoided any conversation about a future like the plague, which was hard to do around his mom.

Connor sent a quick text. Very quick. I wondered what it said. "Piss off" would be a good one.

Kay looked over at me and mouthed, "Be nice."

I wasn't aware that my thoughts could be heard with such clarity.

My dad came in the door. Captain Sean Reid, dressed in his turnout gear, had his neon-yellow helmet tucked under his arm and a scowl plastered across his face.

"Good evening, sir," Connor said. The two men shook hands before Connor reached under the counter and produced another shot glass.

"Are you girls alright?" Dad's voice was gruff.

"I'm good." My father brought out that southern girl in me. He made me want to slip on a pair of well-worn cowgirl boots and jump in the back of the pickup truck to go fishing. Seeing him brought back just that sense of comfort, and also a big dose of ruh-roh. He'd have my hide if he knew I was heading to a graveyard at midnight to watch horny (in every sense of the word) unicorns prancing in the moonlight.

My dad had given me a starter kit in life: never take shit from anyone; being a female should never be a barrier; beauty is internal, not external; and, it's your life, your rules. I didn't understand that then. It took a long time and heartbreak to embrace what he meant, but when I got it, I was much happier.

Though I made sure to keep my private life private, out

of respect, just like he did when I was a kid–he sheltered me, and I tried to do the same.

I was glad Kay and I were back in our work clothes. Maybe it was dark enough in the alley and there was enough commotion that he hadn't noticed my earlier get-up. I crossed my fingers behind my back.

Still, the scowl was upsetting.

"I'm on duty, but thanks," he said to Connor before turning back to me. "I got concerned, that's all. When the call came in that Bobbi Jax was down a dark alley, and you all needed an ambulance, you can imagine what that would do to an old man's heart."

I knew that feeling. Over the years, I'd listened to the emergency channel on the radio and wondered if everyone left unscathed from the latest three-alarm fire. "You're a spring chicken, dad. You're only fifty-eight." Which reminded me that Felicia's fiancé and my dad were the same age.

Once again, I had to swallow down a little slick of sick that floated up my throat. "We're safe and sound. Kay was playing the mama bird, making all the requisite calls, even if she wasn't great at giving clear information."

He grinned at that. "How are you doing, Kay?"

"I'm good. Busy though, keeping Bobbi Jax out of trouble."

Dad knocked his knuckles on the counter to signal his departure. He nodded his head, and waved goodbye. We turned back to the glasses in front of us. We tapped them on the bar three times for good luck, then tossed the whiskey back before coming up sputtering.

My phone buzzed with a text. Ben Johnson.

Johnson: **Heard you're a hero. Can I buy you a drink?**

Me: **Not tonight. I need to go home and sterilize myself. It's not every day I roll around in an alley. Care to pick me up?**

Johnson: **You need a ride home? I can't get there 'til end of shift. That ok?**

Me: **Yes, thanks.**

Johnson: **Are you going to show me your mouth-to-mouth skills?**

Me: **Sure, if you'll show me your rolling around skills.**

Johnson: **Good. I was afraid that when I couldn't get back to you, I'd blown it.**

Me: **Blowing it is my job ;)**

Johnson: **Ha!**

Johnson was fun to play with. His mind worked along the same line mine did–bawdy as hell.

Twinkles's whine interrupted my texting. His stomach grumbled loudly. I made a stink face at Kay. "Damned unicorn poop."

"What's that?" Connor asked.

"Twinkles got into some sparkles and it isn't sitting well."

"I saw that a second ago. Have you taken up crafts all of a sudden?"

"Um, no. Kay, you want to walk with me?"

Kay looked over at Connor. "How about I stay back and watch the bar, and Connor can go with you? He's wearing his uniform. It should keep the Death Eaters at bay."

Connor looked suspicious as I grabbed a plastic bag and Twinkles's lead. "Death Eaters?" he asked.

I shrugged. "Something Marley said."

"Marley?"

"Yeah, the old guy at the cemetery."

He frowned, but remained quiet.

We headed out the door and meandered back in the same direction we'd walked earlier. Once Twinkles had christened, or in this case bedazzled, a spot, he liked to make sure his scent firmly staked his claim. So I knew where we were headed.

Connor slid his hands in his pockets, and we walked in companionable silence. We glanced down the alley, where Dick was taking a picture. Dick used to have his name at the top of my bunny-hop dance card. He'd recently been promoted to detective and no longer wore a blue uniform. As much as I tried, I just didn't get the same down-south happy feelings when he was in a dress shirt and tie.

"BJ," he called.

Connor and I stopped at the top of the alley. I needed to talk to Dick about being on my promotional calendar. He had the kind of hard muscles that would be a great contrast for a fluff ball puppy.

Dick came toward us with an evidence bag in hand. "Hey, we found something I want you to take a look at."

We moved under the streetlight.

With gloved hands, he reached in the bag and pulled out a beautiful old-fashioned piece of jewelry. "Does this belong to you?"

"Is it a pocket watch?" I asked.

He snapped it open, revealing the inside of a locket with three little curls of hair each tied with a slim satin ribbon, two pinks, one blue. On the top was engraved a monogram – a capital R surrounded with a R and a J.

"That's a hell of a coincidence," I said. My legal name was Roberta Jacqueline Reid.

Dick snapped it closed. "Not yours, then?"

I wished it were. The cover was encrusted with tiny semi-precious jewels and the diamond in the center must have been at least a carat. "Sadly, no. You found it in the alley?" I pulled out my phone. "Can I take a picture?"

"I don't see why not." Dick looked back toward the alley. "We were looking for something to identify the woman that you helped. Congratulations. That was really heroic, BJ." He swung his gaze toward me and he had a little puppy love shining in them that made me feel a combination of guilt, and also like I'd done well to cut him off when I did. Angel. Devil.

"Right time, right place, right dog," I countered with a shrug. Twinkles was lying at my feet, panting. I reached a hand down and rubbed behind his ears. He moaned a little to thank me. And then his stomach groaned a little, just 'cause. Unicorn poop.

Dick shot me a questioning look.

"It's the glitter," I said. "So what happens to the locket now?"

"I take it to the lost and found. They'll do a computer check to see if anyone put it on a list–stolen goods. When the lady is coherent, I'll go in and ask around the subject to see if it might not be hers. If she can describe it, we'll hand it back. If it's not hers then there's a waiting period, then we'll put it up in the auction to help families of our cops who are hurt or killed in action."

I looked over at Connor and frowned. I hated that the two men I loved most in this world, Connor and my dad, were both in jobs that put them in life-threatening situations every single day.

With that, Twinkles had had enough. He jumped up and started down the sidewalk. I raised my hand in salute.

"That's my cue. Hey, I need to talk to you about a project I'm working on. Mind if I text you later?"

"Yup. Always glad to hear from you, BJ," Dick said.

Twinkles yanked me down the road. "See you later," I called over my shoulder.

Again, we walked in silence. Connor scratched a hand over his chin that was sprouting a five o'clock shadow that, I can't lie, did really nice things for his face.

"That's a really odd coincidence that the locket had your initials. It looked ancient. I think that the whole 'locket with the hair' thing was something they did before the Civil War. What folks kept before there were photographs."

"I heard that when they did get cameras, it was so expensive that they could only afford to take picture of their dead children. The photographer would pose them on stands like mannequins, with the live children circling in to the frame. They'd take their photos all together."

"That's morbid as hell. Can you imagine having to sit there with your dead sibling?" Connor made a stink face. "You can't be serious."

"Serious. Nasty but serious."

Speaking of nasty, Twinkles couldn't make it to his pooping spot. He was out in front of us. squatting on the sidewalk. I had never seen him do that before, and I got worried that my earlier Googling had given me the wrong information about the effect of marshmallows.

I pulled out my bag and waited. And waited. And waited.

Twinkles took a few more staggering, hunched steps forward and let go of another soft-serve. This time it included a swirl of purple. "Mrph, I wondered where those panties had gone."

Connor pulled up a flashlight app and pointed it at the glittering mound. "You know what that reminds me of?"

"I can't even imagine." I handed the lead to Connor so I could clean up the mess. "Stop looking at it–those are my panties."

"Funnily enough, they don't do a thing for me when they're lying on the sidewalk after a trip through Twinkles's GI track." I heard laughter in his voice as I tucked my hair back and went in for the scoop.

"Have you ever seen the YouTube advertisement for efficient pooping?" I was down on a knee, trying to be efficient myself.

"The British chick who wants to spray the toilet water before you release Zeus's thunder and leave a Roman numeral II?"

"No, I'm talking about the guy in the Renaissance outfit who talks about unicorn poop, and then they pan over to the kids eating rainbow-colored ice cream cones."

"Ha, no. What's it an advertisement for?"

"Something to put your feet on when you're on the throne."

"I don't get it."

"It makes you squat more naturally."

He grinned down to where I was squatting on the sidewalk and winked. I elbowed him the best I could. I got his shin. "Hey!"

"Hey, what?"

"Bring that flashlight closer." I lifted my chin towards my progress.

"I thought you didn't want me seeing that you wear lavender lace thongs."

"They're in the bag. Stop giving me a hard time."

"Let me guess, that's your job, right?"

"Funny, but inappropriate." After I'd scooped, I'd realized there was something left behind that was solid. Man-made solid, not a dog-made solid. Not a natural part of something that should be shooting out the back end of my dog.

Connor pulled a pair of nitrile gloves from his tool belt. He reached down and picked it up.

"What is it?"

"A ring. Are you missing one of your rings?"

"I don't know. Hard to tell from that. I'll wash it off back at the bar." Which was the direction that Twinkles had taken off in.

Connor pulled his glove inside out as he held the ring, making a handy little carrier which he neatly tied off. "I've never seen a dog live up to his name better than Twinkles does."

Twinkles turned to look around and I could swear he gave Connor a wink, then continued to trot forward with a new little jig in his step. He must have been feeling better.

CHAPTER SIX

I WAS BACK at the bar when a cop car pulled up to the front. It was two-thirty in the morning. I didn't think today was going to end. The birds would be singing soon.

"There's Ben," Connor said. "I'm taking Kay home." He leaned over and kissed my nose, gave my ponytail a tug, and moved to open the door as Kay emerged from the back room.

"Kay, I'm so sorry for all this. You have to be at work in a few hours."

She sidled over to give me a hug good-bye. "I'm going to call in sick to work tomorrow. Well, today."

"Why?" I held her in place. "What's wrong?"

"Nothing. I need to catch up on my sleep and be well-rested if we're going on a unicorn safari tonight. But what I'm going to tell Mr. Cheatham is that I've got my period, and I have horrible cramps bending me in two. By the time I sound out 'puh', he'll be shushing me and telling me to take the rest of the week off. He's got some kind of phobic reaction."

"Might be why he hasn't got a wife."

"Yeah, that and the fact that his husband might object."

"That could be it too." I waved as she hustled out the door Ben Johnson was holding open for her.

After she'd left, Johnson turned the key in the lock, then headed my way with a twinkle in his eye. I was happy to see his athletic build, his handsome face. *Whew. Yes, indeed.* I blew a whistle of appreciation. "Looking mighty fine in your blues, officer." He was another prime candidate for the calendar. And I'm sure he'd say yes to please me.

Dick, Connor, and Johnson – only fifteen more hard bodies to get my hands on, so to speak. And since these guys didn't need to be on my bunny list, it wouldn't be wrong for me to look at the boys in blue who were already in relationships. The more I thought about it, the more I was liking Felicia's idea.

"Communications said you had something to show me." He took two paces toward me, and I could see the devil was lighting up his eyes. His gaze travelled down my body. The air between us sizzled.

I wriggled to adjust to the sudden flow of hormones through my system. I still felt a little gross from the alley scene. I had hoped to do a little primping before he'd gotten here. "You came quicker than I expected," I said.

He caught my gaze and shook his head. "That is something I'd never want to do."

Mmm mmm mmm, yep, he was up to no good, which was fine by me. "Officer Johnson, I called Communications and asked for you. You are here on official business," I said as if offended.

"Okay, officially," he stood up straight, puffed out his chest, tucked his chin at attention, "How would you like me to protect and serve?"

"In just that order. First protection, then servicing." I smiled, and he leaned in for a kiss.

He crossed his arms and rested his elbows on the counter that kept us apart.

"It just might be, officer," I blinked my lashes, "in fact it is highly probable, that I've hidden evidence on my body."

"Hmmm, I can't allow that to happen, ma'am. First, I'll need to frisk you. And if I can't find the evidence, I'm afraid I'll have to give you a strip search."

"That's just what I'd hoped for." I swung my hips off toward my office, and Johnson hustled to join me. He showed me what I'm assuming is the proper policing technique for a pat down.

I was pretty darned sure that he hadn't missed the blue nitrile glove in my pocket the first several times his hands felt over the top of my clothes – all the way down the outside of my legs, all the way up the inside of my legs, front and back. Then my arms, now my torso. He was doing a pretty good job making sure there was nothing hidden in my bra.

"Official business," I repeated over and over. Okay it sounded more like a moan than an actual reminder, but I was trying. "Come on." I wriggled to catch his attention. If he kept this up, I wasn't going to stop and show him the ring. Then he'd be off duty, and I didn't want to tell the story to a different police officer who might not be quite so understanding. "That's enough, Officer Johnson. Head in the game," I said sternly.

"Get my head in the game? Yes, ma'am." He reached for his belt.

I nodded with a slow smile and a wag of the finger.

He sighed, settled back on the office sofa, and held out the palm of his hand. I placed the bundle on top.

"What is it?"

"It's a poop-covered ring."

He looked down at it. Looked back at me. Blinked. I thought that was probably disbelief I read in his eyes.

He cleared his throat. "You were digging in poop and found a ring?"

"I was cleaning up after my dog," I smiled sweetly, "as is required by city ordinance, and found the ring."

He untied the glove, opened it up and looked in. Then turned his head away with the exact same look that Connor gets when Ashley was calling. He closed the glove back up, and stood. "It was lying under the poop?"

"No, I believe it was fully processed."

"And I'm assuming it's not your ring."

Johnson headed toward the bathroom and I followed along behind. "I don't wear rings. Especially not one that is that big. I don't really wear jewelry."

"Except pearl necklaces." He turned and winked

"On special occasions," I smiled as I caught his gaze. "Okay, what should I do with it?"

"Let's start by cleaning it off and making sure it didn't come out of a gumball machine."

"Feels too heavy for that."

He put a paper towel in the sink. "Do you have some food prep gloves?"

I ran off to fetch him a pair. First, he swished the ring through the toilet bowl water to get it mostly free of attachments. "Twinkles is pooping glitter?"

"He's special that way. Magical, really," I said after the flush had quieted.

"You don't think that's toxic for dogs?"

"It came from the unicorn poop he was licking." I turned the faucet as hot as I thought Johnson could stand it and squirted some hand soap on the ring. "I don't think they have unicorn poop listed at the poison control site for dogs. Google, though, says I shouldn't let him have it, even if it is non-toxic."

"Unicorn poop? You went to the cemetery?"

"I was trying to bring some lunch to Marley." I stood behind him but we could see each other in the mirror as he cleaned the ring. "But I couldn't find him. Twinkles was a lot more successful at what he was hunting for. Are you going to tell me about the unicorns? Did you find them?"

"I did. It was entertaining, I'll give you that much."

"Were they as horny as Marley said they were?"

He shook the ring and turned off the faucet. "They each had a horn. Maybe that's what he was talking about. I personally didn't see them mating in the cemetery. They were kind of running around and dancing to medieval music. They had ribbons that they were dancing with. I didn't see any laws being broken, but I was there less than five minutes." He turned and leaned his hips against the sink.

I nodded. "Rough night?"

"Yeah. Things were a little out of hand around the city. Happens every full moon." He held the ring up between us.

Holy freaking moly! Holy freeeeaaaakkkking moly!

"That's an emerald and those are diamonds. That ring must be worth a gazillion dollars!"

He turned it around and scrutinized it under the light. "Yeah, that's about the assessment I'd give it."

"What are you going to do with it now? Does it go in lost and found?" I pulled out my phone to take a picture of it.

"This might need to be investigated to see if it's reported on any stolen property lists. Usually if someone loses something of this value they've called the cops to file a report so they can claim it on their insurance."

"Will you keep me abreast of any information?" I batted my lashes at him.

His eyes descended to my chest. "I'd be happy to." His eyes came up, and he took a step forward.

I waggled a finger at him. "You're in the middle of a case, officer. You need to take the ring in and clock out." I peeked at the time. "Can you come back here as soon as you're done? I'm not one hundred percent sure that you found everything that needed to be found when you were searching me."

"Well, I patted you down as best I could." He studied me for a moment, then lifted his brow. "The next step would have to be the strip search, I'm afraid."

A smile spread across my face. "Funny, I'm not afraid at all."

CHAPTER SEVEN

I RARELY WAKE up thinking in Jeopardy clues. This morning, I woke up to "Things that go bump in the night for a hundred, Alex." And it wasn't the good kind of nighttime bumping either. In my dream, poor Alex T. was ducking from the ghouls overhead, stepping carefully around unicorn poop, and swatting away the second-hand smoke that Marley was generously blowing in his direction. I sniffed hard.

Smoke?

That was definitely smoke. I leapt from my bed and ran to my kitchen where I found my coffee pot had come on automatically, but I had failed to fill the reservoir with water, and things were overheating.

My engines were revved enough without the caffeine. Seems adrenaline is aces at getting the whole system jolted awake. I would have slept longer, too. Ten o'clock by most people's standards was sleeping in, but for me, I hadn't hit the hay–to sleep—until four this morning. Johnson did his best to prove he was one of Jamesburg's finest. And he was.

Fine, I mean. I headed into the shower with a big old smile across my face.

Twinkles popped an eye open and then shut it again. Too early, he seemed to say. He chomped the air, then settled back to sleep. I'd take him for a walk as soon as I could get myself together.

Maybe we'd head over to the little park in front of the police station so I could scope out possible models for my all-purpose calendar to benefit Hooch's, the cops, and the puppies. It made me feel all warm and fuzzy just to think of all the good we would do.

All right, I felt all warm and fuzzy because I'd have to be on the shoots with the cops and I'd get to check them out personally. I knew quite a few guys I could ask, but for this particular project I didn't have to confine myself to free-range officers. As long as I was looking and not touching, I could ask the guys who were dating or even married to participate. Surely their wives wouldn't say no to such a wonderful project.

By the time I had swiped on some mascara and a little lip gloss, pulled a brush through my hair, and slipped my feet into my tennis shoes, Twinkles was ringing the bells on the doorknob, letting me know it was time to go out. I wondered if he'd produce any new surprises in this morning's constitutional.

He was unusually compliant on the lead today. He meandered over to his favorite stop sign and watered the three blades of grass that valiantly clung to life in the otherwise dry soil. Then we trotted down the road in the direction of the cop park.

Twinkles lay at my feet, sniffing at the squirrels and panting. I sat on the bench, watching the officers come and go, trying not let my own panting be quite as obvious as

Twinkles's. My gaze caught on a particularly marvelous length of officer as he walked past the park and up the road. I swiveled my head to keep him in view and watched as he walked to a coffee shop on the other side of Gottlieb Family Jewelers.

How very convenient, I thought as I got to my feet.

First stop, coffee. And a brush-by with the stellar-looking officer. Six-foot three, brilliant blue eyes. Whew! Gold ring on his left finger. Mrph. But still, I read the name off his tag: Officer Goodman. I just bet he was, too, I thought, taking in the size of his shoes. Too bad I'd never find out.

I pulled out my phone and texted the name to myself and then I took his picture when he stopped outside to pet Twinkles, who was being an unexpectedly good boy and letting the nice officer scratch his ears for him. I got a little worried about that. Twinkles wasn't usually helpful. I smiled at Goodman. He smiled back. Pearly white teeth, dimple on one side. Oh, dear god, why did you have to find him a wife? Maybe it was a husband? I shrugged and went back inside, where my coffee was waiting on the counter.

Twinkles had crawled under the shade of the bench and looked perfectly content. I brought him some water in his folding bowl. I set that down next to him, took a gulp of coffee, and went into the jewelers to see what kind of stud muffin Stewart Bartholomew the V could be to have snapped up a cute little twenty-something like Felicia.

"Hello," I said with the door bells jingling over my head.

A thin-lipped smile in a rather anemic looking face greeted me. I looked around the counters, then peeked toward the door.

"Is there something special that you're looking for?"

"Actually, I was looking for Mr. Gottlieb. Is he in?"

"I am Stewart Gottlieb." Okay, no. Just... no. "I'm sorry, I'm looking for Stewart Gottlieb the V," I said, as I was sure this must be the ninety-six-year old in excellent shape rather than the fifty-year old looking like the crypt keeper. *Please?* I stuck my fingers behind my back and crossed my fingers for a little burst of make-it-so juju.

"Yes, Stewart Gottlieb the V. How may I be of service?"

Well, first I had to swallow down the bile that crawled up my throat as I remembered Felicia rubbing her stomach and talking heirs and spares. Good grief. You know, everyone has their *thing*.

For me, it was cops and badges.

For the horny unicorns romping in the graveyard it was–something medieval and glittery-magical.

And for Felicia? Well, I couldn't put my finger on the specific thing that might rock her socks–pasty old guys with greasy comb-overs? The smell of denture cream? Ugh.

I finally had my throat clear enough to say, "I'm friends with Felicia, and she told me about your engagement." I turned and looked out the window to check on Twinkles, who was fine, and turned back. "I was getting a coffee next door and thought I'd slip in and introduce myself."

His face made no shift of friendliness. He made no sign of welcome. He actually kind of reminded me of a guy who should work at a funeral parlor. Stewart was giving me the creeps.

I glanced back at Twinkles. Twinkles had rolled onto his back, sunning his belly, his tongue drooping lazily out the side of his mouth. If this guy was trouble, Twinkles would know and come to my rescue, right? As I turned back, I thought what an odd, out-of-the-blue thought that had been. And I squelched it.

I reached in my pocket and pulled out my phone. "Also,

I was wondering if you might look at two pictures of pieces of jewelry and tell me what you think."

He exhaled a long sigh that smelled like Brussel sprouts and butterscotch. He shook his head. "I cannot ascertain anything about a piece of jewelry from a phone picture. The size, the quality of stones, all of that requires me to look at it very carefully in person."

"I don't have them in person to show you." I tried to smile warmly, but I didn't think I pulled it off. "I'm more looking for a general idea about their design. One of them seems very old and the other newer, but still old."

"What did you say your name was?"

"I'm BJ. Felicia and I went to school together in high school, and now she's picking up some hours in the bar I manage until she finds another marketing job."

"Yes, she mentioned you to me." He fluttered his hand in a come-here gesture, but I stood my ground, just reaching the phone out to him, queued up to show the image of the necklace.

"My, my, my. Yes. Yes, indeed." His eye was nearly touching the screen.

I would have suggested to him that I could make the image larger for him. But he seemed comfortable enough, and I could probably swab the screen off with an alcohol wipe from the first-aid kit at the bar.

"This is a piece that was designed in the mid-nineteenth century, just prior to the war of Northern Aggression."

"Northern Aggression?" I asked. *Seriously?*

"Indeed. It was designed for a woman by the name of Rosemary Joselin Ruthington, an old and distinguished Virginian family. The last of the Ruthington line recently passed away—a lovely woman by the name of Opal Ruthington. She was in her late nineties when she passed."

He looked up suddenly and all my blood drained to my feet. I felt like I'd been caught shoplifting. "How did you come to take a picture of this piece?"

"How did you come to know so much about this piece?" I countered.

"My great-grandfather designed it right here in this shop. Our family has been in business here for almost as long as this has been a city, and we know all the great families and their pieces. This one," he picked up a pen and tapped my screen, "I am familiar with the locket because Opal was buried with it. "

"Recently?" I asked.

"Yes, this past Saturday, as a matter of fact."

"Oh, well, then it can't be the same piece." I was mildly disappointed. It would have been cool to tell Dick where the necklace belonged.

"I cleaned the piece prior to her burial myself. I am very sure that this is Opal's great-grandmother's locket. It contained the curls of three of the great grandmother's children taken by scarlet fever in the 1800s. Two girls and a boy. And her initials were inside."

Ruh roh. It was the same necklace. But how...? "That's so interesting that you knew what jewels she was to be buried with. Is that customary?"

"For our establishment, it is. One of the services we offer is to go to our good families' homes once a year and clean their jewels, offer appraisals if their values have increased, and check for any repairs that needed to be made."

"Such as..."

"Prongs that aren't holding the stone securely, for example." He licked his lips and I wondered how he kissed when they were so thin and white. Then I got a flash of Felicia kissing him. I needed to avoid those images.

"But you asked about burial. With our older clientele, they have their outfits picked out in advance and have left notes for the funeral parlor. The funeral parlor contacts us and as a service to our better clients, we clean and place the jewelry once they are resting comfortably in their caskets so they look just so at their viewing."

"Then the family takes off the jewelry before burial?" Dick said the necklace was very expensive.

Gottlieb looked offended.

I raised my brow.

"The jewels that are chosen go with the deceased."

"And if it's not written down?"

"Well, then I help the bereaved make the choice based on my knowledge of the families' history and my client's personal preferences."

"Did Opal choose her jewels?"

He laid a delicate hand on his heart. "It was I who made the selection for dear Miss Ruthington."

I wrinkled my nose. "You can't take jewels to heaven, you know. They're just kind of in the box with a dead body." I pointed out what I thought was darned obvious. I mean heck, that jewel-encrusted locket could probably do a lot of good if auctioned off for the right charity. It did no good at all six feet under.

Stewart's lashes fluttered as he rolled his eyes. I thought he might be having a seizure. "No, dear." He realigned his gaze. "The families who have this kind of a jewelry collection do not need to be so miserly as to take them off their dead relatives."

"I see. Huh." I didn't see at all. I was trying to wrap my brain around all of this. If the necklace was in the casket with Opal, then how did the bag lady having a heart attack have it next to her in the alley? I thought about Twinkles's unexpected expulsion of the emerald ring. It had to have been discarded on the ground somehow for him to have eaten it.

Then it hit me like a boulder. *Death Eaters.*

CHAPTER EIGHT

I TOOK another quick look out the window at Twinkles lying under the coffee shop bench, and he looked comfortable. Though, quite honestly, if he wasn't happy and I had to leave this creepy-as-shit store, it would be just fine.

I glanced around. It wasn't a creepy-as-shit store. It was a lovely store. Posh, even. The walls were made of coffered cherry. Underfoot was a beautiful oriental rug. There were cases of gleaming gems. There was a little antique dressing table where a lady might sit and examine her reflection while trying on earrings and necklaces. Over to the side, away from the sun, a seating area had delicate chairs and a china tea service set out. I imagined that this was a lovely spot for ladies to enjoy while they shopped. It seemed welcoming, especially if Gottlieb's clientele was the age of Opal Ruthington.

No, it wasn't the space that gave me the heebie-jeebies. I had no idea why I was so creeped out. Could be that my original visualizations when I met him—the ones where Stewart the Crypt Keeper was French-kissing Felicia—set the wrong tone. Another image popped into my imagination—his veiny hands cupping Felicia's boob. My stomach dropped, and I was glad I hadn't eaten today. Gross. I took in a deep breath. I needed my mind to go elsewhere. "That's such a lovely service you provide. Do the various funeral homes call you? How does that work?"

"Most of the better families only use Greenspoon Funerary Services. Our clientele come from the same fine Virginian stock."

"Of course." I nodded my agreement and wondered if Felicia's DNA produced the kind of blood this guy seemed to hold in such high esteem. I didn't think so. And it seemed a bit off that he'd taint the family line with lesser-quality lineage.

But what did I know? Maybe the bluebloods were all taken or barren or had better eyesight than Felicia did. Maybe Gottlieb was forced to reach down to the farm league to find someone to play ball with him. Damn. Another image flashed into my imagination, and it took everything I had to keep from grimacing.

Stewart moved toward the back room and waved for me to follow. Which I did. Reluctantly.

"You see?" He opened a large scrap book. Above the desk was a shelf lined with similar books. "Here. Here is Opal's obituary. I look at the death notices every morning, cut out the ones of importance and mount them in my archive."

"Over breakfast? You *eat* over *death* notices?"

"Yes, exactly. I have my morning meal whilst perusing the paper, and I pay extra close attention to the notices, looking for my customers' names. Just this last week, I have lost three of my clientele from my better families. Each needed my attention in preparing for their long journey home."

The telephone rang, and he turned away. "Please excuse me for a moment."

I flipped to the front page. It was a woman named Evelyn Chiles. I snapped a picture, then I took a photo of Opal's obituary and four others before I heard Stewart hanging up the phone in the front room. I stood up and tried not to look guilty. I decided not to show him the picture of the ring, thinking it was a better idea for me to skedaddle.

"Nice to meet you," I said as I moved toward the front room and then toward the door. "I left my dog outside and I need to finish his walk."

"Oh? But I have questions for you. How did you come upon a picture of the Ruthington locket?" he asked as I pushed through the door.

I pretended not to hear him and skittered over to the happily recumbent Twinkles, whose belly was being scratched by the coffee guy. The coffee guy was kinda cute, I thought. Too bad he didn't have a badge. Cute only went so far in my book. I needed something more to wet my whistle—so to speak.

I roused Twinkles and let him lap down some water before I shook out the bowl, put it back in the little pouch on his lead, and headed off to Kay's office to see if she wanted to get an early lunch.

Twinkles and I meandered toward Do-we, Cheat'em and How, which is what Kay called the law office where she works. Mr. Cheatham, Esq. thought it was the funniest thing ever. At least he had a sense of humor about his business ethics. As Twinkles and I traced our way up the block, turning at the cop park, I thought about the large ring that Felicia wore on her left hand.

They must be in love, Stewart and Felicia. Must be. I've heard of gold diggers trying to marry into money and getting their hooks into some dude with one foot in the grave. But that had been kind of a nebulous tabloid thing. Now that I saw it in person... that wasn't really fair. Stewart and my dad were the same age. My dad was far from the grave. I crossed my fingers to give that thought a little extra good juju. Stewart, though...I never would have guessed he was in his fifties. I'd mistaken him for *his* father, after all.

Yup. Felicia had to be in love for some reason or another because to do that man for profit? I got a whole-body shiver at the thought. I walked some more, replaying the whole scene in the jewelry shop. I had to tell Kay about this shit.

I mean, what were the chances that a person's jewelry made its way from the dead body in a casket to next to a dying woman in the alley?

Dick said he was going to talk to the bag woman about the locket. I needed to call Dick to see if he could tell me what happened to that lady. *Should I tell him that I think I know who owned that locket?* Hmm. Maybe. Maybe not.

If I told Dick that the locket belonged to dead Opal, then he might have to go investigate her grave. If he did that, it might just scare away the unicorns, and I darned well wanted to see the unicorns. Okay, I'd tell Dick after tonight. It would be just a few hours extra. What difference could a few hours make?

I turned the corner and walked east.

That locket was, by Stewart Gottlieb's own admission, something of great value. Stewart was one of the last people, if not *the* last person, to touch it. I chewed on my lip. He kept books of obituary notices. How strange was that? He must have decades of obituaries in those scrap books.

My body gave one of those unaccounted-for tremors. The childhood phrase popped up in my mind: "Someone must have walked on my grave." Like I did yesterday, tiptoeing through the cemetery, trouncing on dead people. "Sorry! So sorry," I whispered toward the sky, in case I picked up a hitchhiker ghost. You never knew. You couldn't be too careful about these things.

My stomach growled. I needed something to eat. Which got me back on the Death Eater track. What in the heck was a Death Eater? I had no clue. But I knew someone who did.

I decided to get some lunch to take to Marley.

BJ: Are you up for some adventure? I texted Kay.

My father taught me that there are two kinds of people in this world: cowards that run from fear, and heroes who feel the fear and race toward the problem anyway. Just like there was a difference between cowardice and heroism, there was also a difference between stupid and not quite as dumb. I needed backup–just like any good cop, as heroic as they were. I didn't want to head to the cemetery on my own. I mean, Twinkles was badass when it came to eating bad guys, but how much support would he be around ghouls?

It didn't take long for my phone to beep back.

Kay: **What's up?**
BJ: **Graveyard. Hunt for Marley.**
Kay: **Come by and get me.**

WITH A GREASY BAG filled with piping hot fries and

three cardiac-arrest burgers, Kay and I walked under the cemetery arch.

"We tried down the right-hand path last time, so let's try the left now." I pointed toward the ground, where there was a trail of hoof prints in the dirt patch beside the sidewalk.

"And glitter," Kay said with a lift of her chin. "Better hold tight to Twinkles's lead."

I wrapped the leather around my hand an extra turn, though I also thought that would do less to keep Twinkles by my side than set me up for a very rough ride if he caught a scent that was enticing and took off, dragging me behind him. I hoped the three burgers I fed him at the restaurant had filled his belly to a point that he could pass up unicorn poop for dessert.

"Marley," I called. "Marley, I brought you some lunch." We were at the top of the hill, and my voice carried out across the cemetery. I caught movement on the next hill over. A flash of hot pink.

I pointed in that direction and Kay waved her arms over her head. "We're over here!" she called. "We brought you some food."

A nimble man with a grey ponytail and kaleidoscope-colored clothes came bounding our way.

"That was easier than I expected," I said as we made our way in his direction.

"Food is a powerful motivator—we weren't yelling about food last time."

"True." We all slowed our paces to figure out the situation. "Marley?"

"Ma'am," he said, snapping to and giving me a salute.

"I'm BJ, and this is my friend Kay." Kay gave him a finger waggle. "And Twinkles." I nodded my head toward Twinkles who seemed to pick up on the military stance

Marley had affected and was sitting at attention in a line with Kay and me. "A friend of mine, Officer Johnson, told me that you lived here and that you heroically stopped a war between the unicorns and Death Eaters. I thought I would invite you to lunch with us, and you might tell us about that night."

Marley's eyes slid to my bag. His breathing became short and shallow, but he pulled himself back into proper military attention. "It would be an honor."

Kay handed him one of the sodas. And I handed him the bag. All of it. My growling belly was a first-world problem. I could make a PB and J at my place. I wasn't sure when Marley had last eaten. Kay didn't bat an eye at the decision.

We all sat on the grass while Marley ate. Kay lounged back, using Twinkles as a pillow, and I picked grass impatiently.

"The Death Eaters have never been out on a full moon before," Marley said as he chewed, swiping at his chin with a paper napkin. "Wonder why they decided to come this time."

"Have there always been Death Eaters in the cemetery?" Kay asked.

"Nah, just here in the last six months or so. Used to be quiet. Nice place for the unicorns to play. Lots of space and quiet so they could do their breeding."

"The unicorns have been here for longer?"

"Ever since I got here. That was like four, maybe five winters ago when I moved in to the mausoleum." He pointed to a far hill where I could just make out the peak of a roof. "Cold in there in the winter. I have to pile up my clothes to get me off the marble. But it mostly keeps me out of the elements. Sometimes I build me a fire and the marble can get nice and toasty. Can't always keep it going, though. Not enough fuel around these parts."

I nodded knowingly. I'd had my fair share of nights around a campfire with Hooch and my dad when the fuel ran out before the night did. Those could be some cold nights. "Thickens the blood," Hooch would say.

Marley took a loud slurp of soda and closed his eyes, as if relishing the bubbles running down his throat.

"So now I'm curious as to why the Death Eaters and unicorns would be out on the same night for the first time," Kay said.

Marley popped his eyes back open. "Probably because they'd just put a body in the ground the day before. The ground is easy to dig into. It's easy to get down in there and feast on the fresh meat."

He took a big bite out of the hamburger, and I winced. I wondered about what Johnson said about Marley and PTSD. Was this a flashback from something he saw in the war? Was this a past acid trip?

"The grass comes in rolls. The groundskeeper waits for all the mourners to be out of sight, then he pushes the loose soil back in the hole. Makes a mound that he clears off so it's flat. What with the body being in the box, there ain't no reason to mound it up. No decay to drop the soil down into an indentation that would fill with water and call the mosquitoes."

Marley had a faraway look in his eye and sat still as a statue, then snapped back to take another bite of burger. "They take the extra soil off to somewhere else, and they roll out the grass like a carpet. A day or so later the Death Eaters get the smell on the air. They come and roll back the grass and they have a big dog that they use to move the soil. Shiny white teeth. Glowing eyes. Enormous jaws on it." Marley put his burger down and put his elbows together, opening and shutting his hands to show the jaws working. He slurped more soda. "Then one of 'em holds the ankles of the other and they get the lid off. Then, they feast."

"Two, then? Two Death Eaters?"

Marley looked off in the distance. "Two. Yeah. The pair of them. Must be a breeding pair. I bet they got some young'uns somewhere 'cause they put the meat in a bag and take it with 'em. Could be more, though. I don't never get too close. I don't know how fresh they like their meat. I mean," Marley was rubbing his hands up and down his scrawny form, "I don't know for sure that they wouldn't still like their meat at 98.6 degrees. See what I'm saying?"

Kay and I shot each other a look. For real?

I cleared my throat. "The night of the first full moon, before the unicorns got here, there were already Death Eaters in the park?"

"I rapped on the officer's door. He was doing his daily calisthenics in the back seat of his car. Worked up a real sweat, too. He was out of breath when he got out to talk to me." Marley scratched at the bottom of his headband. A fat joint stuck out behind his ear, and I wondered if he didn't have a benefactor who was supplying him with this form of self-medication. "I should tell him it's better to do exercise where he's got him some more room."

Kay sent me a look. Part horrified, part choking back laughter. I glowered in return.

"The officer cut on his siren and lights, and I stalked the Death Eaters to make sure they vamoosed."

"And had they?" Kay asked.

"Vamoosed enough. I saw them slam the coffin shut." Marley shoved the last bite of the third hamburger in his mouth and sucked up the last drop of the third soda. He licked his lips, then swiped the sleeve of his shirt across his mouth. "Thank you," he said. "That hit the spot." He pointed back over to where Kay and I had walked yesterday, looking for him. "They got their dog to start shoving the dirt back in the hole. I figured they were going to clean up and head off as quick as they could. I reported back, then did another recon. By the time I got back there everything seemed back in place. The dog was gone and one of the Eaters. Another one saw me and started running. I didn't chase it or nothing. I ain't goin' hand to hand with a flesh-eater if I can help it."

"Smart move," Kay said.

"Marley, do you feel like taking a walk? Could you show me the grave?"

"Sure." He stood and swiped a hand across his butt to clear off the grass. "We can cut through here. Just be careful. The unicorns poop all over the damned place, and it's hell to get the glitter off your shoes."

CHAPTER NINE

WE TREKKED down the dirt path. This deep in the cemetery, there was more gravel and dirt than cement. The sun dappled the ground in bright yellow polka dots through the green leaves of the hardwood trees that graced the slopes. It was a beautiful day. The birds were calling. It wasn't spooky at all walking past the graves.

Nope, not at all, I told myself with as much conviction as I could muster.

Then I felt a cold breeze on my neck beneath my ponytail and heard a soft groaning noise. Hunching my shoulders up to my ears protectively, I turned to see Kay with her lips puckered up, leaning in toward me. The second our gaze met, she grinned. I rolled my eyes and rubbed my arms to get rid of the gooseflesh.

I took a couple of big steps to the side and let Kay get in front of me. I was the caboose. The safe place to be in a line of pranksters; the first to go if there was a real-life ghoulie behind me. We sauntered along in silence, lost in our own thoughts. My own thoughts were, *So far, so good. Twinkles hasn't launched himself off on a marshmallow hunt.*

Marley stopped suddenly, sinking down to a squat like a soldier who had spotted the enemy, his fist in a ball up by his ear. A signal that I recognized from the movies as "hold." Kay and I looked left, then right; front, then back. I didn't see anyone or any*thing*. With all this talk of unicorns and Death Eaters, it was hard to imagine what might have caught his eye or painted itself across his imagination. Kay's gaze caught mine. She shrugged. We sank down beside Marley, balancing with our fingers on the pavement.

Marley chewed on his upper lip, then sniffed hard, wiped his nose on the hem of his shirt, and flopped on his belly, his elbows posted under his chest, his hands held in fists. He snaked forward, using his legs to help propel him over the grass.

I was in jeans, so I got down on all fours.

I glanced back at Kay, who was in dress slacks. She gave me the nuh-uh look with a shake of her head.

Twinkles was on his belly next to Marley; they were brothers in arms, crawling side by side. Twinkles had a big grin on his face. I kind of hovered there, not knowing what the heck was going on, wondering if this patch of green had remained unicorn-free.

Marley reached out a hand and picked a four-leaf clover. No. That couldn't be right. I rocked back until I was squatting, then I duck-walked over to him. Not easy in slim-fit jeans. I had to hold my breath as the waistline bit into my abdomen, compressing the space until it was too small for my diaphragm to function. I looked for signs of unicorns, then dropped my knees.

Marley studied the thing pinched between his fingers,

then held it up for my inspection. Son of a gun, he was holding up an emerald earring. The cut and style would be a good match to the ring Twinkles had swallowed yesterday. I pulled out my phone. "Mind if I take a picture of that?"

Marley held it up to his cheek and gave me a checkerboard grin with every other tooth missing and showing up as a black gap. I took one of him to show him, and one that zoomed in on the earring. When I turned the photo his way, he chuckled. "Man, howdy, I look like shit. Like I just done come out of the jungle."

"You don't seem to be surprised to find a piece of jewelry," Kay pointed out. "Do you find them often?"

"Nope. Not often. Every once in a while, if I scout after the Death Eaters. Especially if something startled them. They startle easy. I do too, if you want to know the truth." He chuckled. "The first time I come on them, I scared the shit out of myself. For real. I watched as one of them was walking their dog away. Didn't know it was a dog at the time. Took me a while to figure that one out. Big dog, though. Bigger than a man. Bigger than three men. There was one that was taking the dog away, and the other was rolling the grass back in place. And then a bat flew in front of my face, and I hollered. Woulda scared the shit out of me again," he bumped my arm and grinned, "but I hadn't had much to eat that day."

I wasn't sure how to react to that information. It was sad. But he seemed to think it was funny. I pulled my lips wide and let him interpret it as he may.

Marley slapped his hands together, then shot one of them out in front of him. "The Death Eater took off running. I thought maybe I'd dreamt it. I went back the next day to check it out. The tomb was kind of crookedy. I was hunting around, trying to figure out what I'd done saw. I was looking for tracks. Wanted to see what kind of feet a Death Eater might have."

"Did you find any?" Kay was wide-eyed at the story.

"Naw, it rained that night. Everything got washed away. I found the necklace on the path, though." He tapped beneath his eye. "If you don't learn how to spot shiny things in the jungle, then you won't see the enemy. They sure as hell see you, though. First-come, first-dead kinda scenario. I learned to get real good real quick, finding the shiny."

"When was all this that you saw the big dog?" Kay asked.

"Back around Veterans' day, I was out putting flags on the vets' tombstones for the grave keepers, that's how I remember when it was. Yup–that night. Then the next day, I found me a real pretty necklace."

"What did you do with it? Did you sell it?"

"Nah, put it in my hidey hole for safe keeping. I figure sooner or later someone will realize they let their necklace fall off and come a lookin' for it."

"You don't think the Death Eater dropped it?"

Marley reached back and rubbed the back of his neck. "Now what would a Death Eater need with a necklace? Naw. It was happenstance that I found it. Someone from one of the old families must have dropped it. The clasp was broke. They'll come lookin'. I'll get it back to the right person."

"That was like six months ago," Kay pointed out.

Marley looked at the grass at his feet, contemplating the time lag. "Some people ain't as self-aware as they should be." He looked back up at Kay. "But as expensive as the necklace must be, I'm sure they'll be searchin' for it."

Marley took off his headband, unrolled it, put the earring in, rolled it back up, and tied it back in place. He plucked the joint from between his lips where he'd put it for safekeeping and tucked it back behind his ear.

We walked a little farther.

"Hey, now looky there," Marley said, pointing. "This is a good finding day. Found you and food, found the earring, and now this."

I saw nothing. I wondered if we'd have to crawl over to it again. My knees were feeling bruised and that was kind of a slutty look, so I wouldn't be able to wear that cute little dress I'd picked out for my next bunny hop with Johnson. He was a leg man, for sure. He'd have to settle for skinny jeans and stilettos.

Marley pointed to the bare ground, where I could see a hoof print. His finger drew an imaginary path up in the air. As my line of sight followed, I could just make out a thin path in the overgrown grass that looked like it had been trampled. I followed the finger up until it stopped and pointed at a tree branch, where there was a gleam of light reflecting off metal. If it was another piece of jewelry, it was going to be the find of the century.

We trotted over to find a purple sparkly horse harness. The bit was the reflective surface. "One of the unicorns must have left this behind by accident," I suggested, looking over at Kay. "After a night of unbridled enthusiasm."

"That was damned corny, you need to rein that in." Kay wrinkled her nose.

Marley tugged it off the limb. "My guess is they took it off when they were rutting so as not to get their hooves caught when things got a little wild. Bet they couldn't find it again in the dark."

I smiled, "Marely should know, he's seen the mane event."

"Boo." Kay rolled her eyes.

I opened my mouth but Kay raised her hand. "Stop."

I followed the line of his finger again as it traced a trail out in front of us. A bit farther on, it looked like the grass had been trampled into a wide circle.

"Could have been aliens landed there," Kay suggested.

Marley scratched his chin, and looked like he was contemplating the possibility.

I took a picture of the harness. Proof that I hadn't breathed in hallucinatory fumes left by Marley at the police cruiser Monday night.

Kay looked at her watch, and I knew she was pushing her time limit. She'd need to get back from her lunch break. She was really good at what she did, so the lawyers cut her a lot of slack, but I didn't want to get her in trouble. She was already doing above and beyond, helping me at the bar.

Now, at least, I could check the guilt box on that while I had Felicia on the payroll. And who knew, if this calendar thingy worked out, maybe I'd have to hire several servers. And I could spend my time flirting with the cop population.

Kay sent me a knowing look and a wink. Sometimes, I thought too loudly.

"Marley, you were going to show us the grave?" I tried to prompt him back into action.

He looked at me blankly.

"You were going to show us the grave the Death Eaters visited?"

He shook the harness. "I'll lay it over where they can find it tonight." He slung it over his shoulder.

We were back on the pathway, heading over a hill. This was the older part of the cemetery, where the writing on the acid-rain etched tombstones dating back into the mid-eighteenth century required braille-like abilities to decipher. These were placed on the highest hill of the grounds. I assumed the Gottlieb family must be buried somewhere in the area, alongside their finer Virginian blueblood clientele.

Again, I thought about Stewart's family tradition of burying the jewels was a ridiculous loss. As Kay's mom told me every time I ate at their house when I was a kid, "Finish all the food on that plate. There are children starving in Africa." I didn't make the connection then – I still didn't, but that was the phrase that came up for me. How could they bury jewels when there were children in need? Wasteful.

"That there's the tomb that got messed up for Veteran's Day." Marley pointed down the row of tombs, all lined up like nice, neat soldiers except for one that was drunkenly stumbling forward. I went over and took a picture of it to show to Dick when I told him about the locket.

By the time I was done, Kay and Marley were standing by another tomb three rows over. That one looked fresh and new. Twinkles and I wandered over. I looked down at the carved stone.

I can't say I was surprised that the information came full-circle–this was Opal's grave.

I know where your necklace is, Opal, and it will serve the fallen police officers' families far better than it would serve you.

Maybe I wouldn't tell Dick what I knew, so he wouldn't have to get it back to this family, who didn't seem to care about the worth of their jewels. Just as that thought came fully formed into my head, a black cloud blew over the sun, casting its long dark shadow over us. It seemed that Opal did *not* approve.

Twinkles pulled his lead out of my hand, danced over to the next row, and hid behind a tombstone. I found him there slurping down rainbow-colored marshmallows and glitter from the top of the unicorn poo. I threw my hands in the air. *Well, shit!*

CHAPTER TEN

KAY WAS SITTING at the bar eating nachos. Not the healthiest of dinners, but our selection of bar food was limited to things that could land you in the hospital with a major coronary. The best I could offer her in the way of nutrition were the lemon and lime wedges that filled the garnish boxes.

It was five-fifteen and Kay had walked over to the bar after work. She wanted me to catch her up on my adventure this morning meeting Felicia's fiancé.

"And you didn't tell him about the necklace you found in the alleyway?" She waggled a cheese-covered nacho at me before popping it in her mouth.

"No. He was giving me the willies."

"I thought only Willy gave you the willies. And I thought that was a good thing."

"Excellent thing, as a matter of fact." I picked up the bar towel and tucked it into my apron strings.

"Noted. Where is Officer Williams anyway? He was

the flavor of the month for a while. Now I'm seeing a lot of Ben Johnson."

"Willy's around, but his new schedule makes things tricky. Johnson's schedule fits mine better right now."

"Ah, it's his schedule that's a good fit? Is that what you kids are calling it nowadays? A schedule? Why, in my day, we'd call it a schlong." Kay snorted, and that made us both laugh. She ate a few more chips while I got her a soda. "I think you should consider having Stewart go across to the police department and identify the locket. As a matter of fact, Stewart might be the only one who can identify the locket for sure, and he'd probably need to see it for himself to be one hundred percent sure, creep factor aside. He sounds just awful. I wonder why Felicia is marrying him."

I shrugged. "Creepy is the new thing, I guess."

"So is money, and Felicia always had a thing for the color green."

"No, you're wrong. She enjoys platinum, gold, and diamond." I glanced up to see Dick standing outside Hooch's front door, looking like he was waiting for someone.

"Diamond is not a color." Kay swung around to see what I was looking at.

"And red Kool-Aid is not a flavor, but it's still your favorite."

She stuck out her tongue out at me like she was six years old again just as Dick and a passel of cops made their way inside.

"Actually, Felicia's mom's been sick. I know she's doing everything she can, but there are a lot of bills to pay."

"Her mom's still in treatment?" I asked. "I thought she was doing better."

"She was in remission. Now she's not in remission."

Felicia was an only child, though her mom seemed to love kids. We were always welcome over at their house. "I'm really sorry to hear that," I said. I was a kid raised by a single parent, too. If anything were to ever happen to my dad... Uh-uh, I couldn't go there, even as a hypothetical. And here Felicia was dealing with the reality

I took in a deep breath and turned toward Dick and his friends. "Welcome to Hooch's," I called. "Belly up to the bar, officers, and tell me your poison."

"I lost a bet, so I owe a round of Badge Bunny Booze all around." Dick caught my eye as he said it. If I could read minds, I'd say that Dick set it up so he could lose a bet and bring a group of officers down and get them drinking here. Which I appreciated. A lot. But Dick also had been wearing an "I want more" vibe whenever we were together. It was one of the reasons why I had to stop seeing him. I don't do relationships. I also don't do detectives. So as soon as he handed in his blue uniform and exchanged it for a coat and tie, he went into the friendship corner. I liked Dick being my friend. I liked Dick. But that was as far as I'd let things go.

I set out ten tumblers and put a double shot in each. Might as well get them happy so they'd stick around.

The lanky officer with the pink ears held up his glass. "To Richard, may he always be so damned sure of himself and may he always bolster his braggadocio with a bet backed with Badge Bunny Booze."

"Hear, hear!" They all tossed back gulps and smiled.

I smiled too, because that was the confirmation I needed to know I was right. Dick was humble—except about his sexual prowess, but then again, that wasn't really bragging. He *was* damned good. That Dick got almost a dozen clients into my shop by losing face. That was something.

Shoot. I didn't want him to do that for me. It made me uncomfortable, like I was beholden to him. Though he wasn't asking for anything, I reminded myself before I let the guilt seep too deep into my psyche. I looked at Kay, who was looking at Dick. Kay swung her gaze over to me with her brow raised high in astonishment and an "Oh, girl! You're in trouble now!" expression.

The men fell into clusters, talking excitedly, and Dick leaned against the bar. His eyes were warm and happy. "I went by the hospital today to talk to the lady in the alley. She calls herself Duckie."

"Serious?"

"She's got dementia. I was talking to her when she seemed to think she was four or so. Duckie must have been her nickname when she was a kid."

"She's alive, then. Surely they're not going to turn her back out on the streets with dementia."

"She's not a homeless woman. She walked out of her care facility a couple of weeks ago down in Richmond."

"Richmond? How the heck...?"

Richmond was a good forty-five minutes away by highway, and that was on light traffic days; any other time, when drivers cluttered the road, well, one could sit in traffic a good sixty to eighty minutes. Just depended on who was trying to get to Charlottesville.

"Might have hitched a ride. Might have climbed on a bus."

"But the clothes. All of them. It took me forever to get her undressed enough that I could do CPR."

Dick shook his head. "No clue. But her family was there. They were pretty shaken. They were sure she had died in the woods somewhere near her facility."

"If she thought she was four years old, then she wouldn't have known anything about the necklace."

"She hadn't a clue. Neither did the family."

I debated again whether to tell Dick right away that I had information about who owned the locket. And again, I decided to keep quiet until tomorrow.

Kay came up behind me and gave me a hug. "I'm going to go take a nap. What time are you closing up?" she whispered in my ear.

"I thought I'd leave at one and let Felicia lock up at closing. I'll do the cleanup tomorrow."

"Okay." She kissed my cheek and left.

Dick's eyes turned, scrutinizing. "What was Kay whispering about naps for? What are you two up to?"

"Uhm."

"Don't think that I didn't see that the two of you were dressed head to toe in black yesterday. You're definitely up to something."

Detective Dick, hard at work. I worked on finding an answer that would be truthful and not answer him at the same time. I was let off the hook by Pink Ears asking me what the name of the dog on the wall was. "Fido," I said.

A collective moan went up.

"I'm not married to the name." I smiled.

Dick turned his eyes on me with a funny little something in them. Did that have to do with the painting? No, I think I had something to do with me saying I'm not married. Huh. "Go ahead and pick something better," I called. I'd grapple with Dick's weird energy later.

The guys got serious about finding the perfect name. Jason, one of the officers, pulled out his phone to Google ideas. Jason was a cutie. I needed to put him on the list for the calendar. His gold ring meant that was the only list I could put him on.

"Chase, Flash, Marshall, Sheriff," he read.

That last one got a collective boo. I thought so too. I wasn't a fan of brown uniforms, even if it had a shiny badge over the heart. They were the ones who always brought by the ABC citations on some drummed-up stupidity by my enemy Nicky next door. The shithead.

"Thunder, Trevor, Turbo." The guys were still trying to name the mural.

Dick came around the counter to give me a kiss. His lips held on mine, then he released with a smile. "I miss being your special friend, BJ."

I nodded. I didn't know what to say. We'd had this conversation. He knew my rules. He pulled a credit card from his wallet, and I ran it through the machine.

"But I'm glad to just come and hang out with you. I like being your friend, too." He tugged my ponytail. "I have to go. Have a great evening. And promise me you and Kay are going to stay out of trouble." He took the pen and receipt and signed across the bottom.

"We plan to. Thank you for everything," I said. Dick was a really good guy. If I ever considered a relationship, I would definitely consider him.

As Dick moved through the front door, Jason yelled, "Terminator!"

"Too long. Someone would shorten it to Minnie," someone said.

FELICIA CAME in while they were still debating. She had on a pair of black waitress shoes with tennis socks and a cute little baby doll dress that fluttered around her upper thighs. There was a collective moment of silence in appreciation for Felicia's silky thighs.

"She's engaged," I said, and they went back to their efforts to rename Fido. Now they were debating if it was in fact a boy or girl dog.

"What's that at the bottom of the mural, BJ?" Jason asked.

"A bone," I said.

"Boner, you mean?"

"Yeah, my artist skills aren't where my talents lie." I winked.

There was a Neanderthal whoop and a raise of glasses in my direction.

"Gentlemen as you down the last sips of your prize, I'm starting tabs." I needed them to think of this as an evening at Hooch's, and not just a round bought by Dick's ego.

The bells chimed and a stud muffin of epic quality walked in. I was watching him in the mirror as I prepped a tray of beers. He was six-foot heaven with broad shoulders and a slender waist. Faded jeans hung from his hips and stretched to cover gladiator thigh muscles. Dark brown hair, a lot longer than I liked, was pulled into a short ponytail. Workman's boots. He had "bad boy" written all over him. His gaze scanned over the interior and settled.

I turned to see what he was looking at with that smile on his face.

Felicia.

She smiled back, worked her way over to him, and slid into his arms.

What?

Felicia must have felt my eyes on her back because she turned, red-faced. "BJ," she said, "This is my brother-in-law to be." She looked up at him with adoration in her eyes, then back at me. "He just needed to pass me a message."

He gave me a wink, gave her a pat on the ass, and left.

Uhm, that wasn't the way my family greeted each other. Of course, I didn't have a brother-in-law to be that looked like that.

In my mind, I juxtaposed Stewart with this guy. Uh-uh. There was no comparison. Slap a badge on that guy, and I'd do him at breakfast, lunch, and dinner. Maybe an afternoon snack. Okay, and a midnight snack too. Damn, I was hungry.

I pulled out my phone.

BJ: **I could sure use your assistance right now, officer.**

It didn't take long for a response.

Johnson: **With protection or just serving?**

BJ: **Protection is always first. Then the serving. I'm at Hooch's.**

Johnson: **Ok. Coming.**

Me: **Mmmm. Sorry to hear that. I had plans for you…**

Johnson: **What?**

Johnson: **HA! Okay. I'm ON MY WAY NOW.**

Me: **Back entrance, please.**

Johnson: **I thought you said you didn't do butt stuff.**

Me: **Really? I have a bar filled with officers, and you want to play funny boy in a text?**

Johnson: **Alley door ETA 2.5 seconds.**

I TOLD Felicia I was taking my fifteen-minute break. She went back to serving the good officers, swinging her hips, making the hem of her dress slip up and down her thighs. The men certainly appreciated it. She was lapping up the attention. Again, there was that disconnect with Stewart the V. It wasn't exactly a good feminist's stance, but shoot, if it made her feel happy, use what you've got, girlfriend.

"Hey," one of the guys at a side table said to Felicia as he signed his credit card receipt. "What did the leper say to the prostitute?"

Felicia shook her head as she took the pen and credit card slip back from him.

"You can keep the tip." His buddy slapped the table and donkey brayed.

Felicia smacked the guy across the back of the head. "What the *hell* is wrong with you?" she asked. The officers were doubled over laughing.

Good, I thought, she can handle herself. I washed my hands, took off my apron, gave my hair a fluff and went out the back door.

True to his word, Johnson showed up by the time the door snicked closed behind me. I climbed in his back seat. Johnson showed me how he got a whole calisthenics workout in in fifteen minutes flat. "That was...*Wow*." I smiled and pushed my damp hair out of my face. "That hit the spot."

"I aim to please."

"And please you did, officer."

The radio crackled. "940, we have a drunk and disorderly at 7772 Main Street."

"That's Dollars to Doughnuts," I said as Johnson leaned over the seat to reach for the radio.

"940, copy. I'm en route." He sat back down and

quickly stuffed himself back together. "Sorry, BJ, I need to eat and run."

I leaned over and gave him a kiss. "We both need to get back to work." I opened the door. "See you later."

He had jumped out of his side and was reaching for his front door handle. "Thanks, BJ."

I gave him a little finger wave and off he went, lights and sirens, getting my blood humming again.

CHAPTER ELEVEN

FELICIA DIDN'T LOOK happy about being left at the bar solo, though I pointed out to her that Joe was there cleaning dishes in the back. That didn't seem to cheer her up. True, Joe only spoke Hungarian and charades, with a spattering of Italian that let him share gossip with the dishwasher at my enemy, Nicky Stromboli's next door restaurant. And his dishwasher hated Nicky so we got all the scoop.

Nicky was going after Hooch's, trying to shut us down. Just today Joe discovered that Nicky had invited his friend at the ABC—Alcoholic Beverage Control—over for a free lunch. And Nicky didn't do free. I was geared up to get yet another trumped-up citation. It should be here any day now.

I'd hold off on worrying about keeping our ABC license until I had the citation in hand. And I wouldn't worry about Felicia getting mad that I was leaving her on her own. There were only five people in the place. Surely, she could handle it. This was her job. She signed on for this.

So, I shrugged and left. I was still looking for another

staff member. We were all clear that this was not where Felicia wanted to be. I didn't expect she'd be around much longer. I'd taken out ads in the university paper—maybe I'd get a bite or two from that.

FOR TONIGHT'S UNICORN SAFARI, Kay was driving. I loaded Twinkles into her back seat. He didn't quite fit, so he stuck his head between the front captains' chairs, and let the cool air from the air conditioning fan his face. He closed his eyes and smiled as we drove off, his tongue dripping saliva on her console. Good thing we loved him so much.

This time, we were wearing our normal clothes instead of skulking around in black. We had decided to drive to the spot that Johnson and I had been frolicking in and use the field glasses still on loan from Kay's dad. It was a nice safe distance, close to a crossroad so we had a quick way to get out of Dodge if things got weird. If an officer pulled up and asked what the heck we were doing, we wouldn't look quite as suspicious. And I thought we were pretty safe from Death Eaters.

We pulled up under the wide branches of the ancient oak. We were well-hidden in the shadow of the cemetery wall. Kay put the car into park and looked around. "Here? Really?"

"It was dark and quiet when Johnson stopped. The full moon was glinting off his badge. What's a girl to do?"

"Play Thumper in the back seat."

Now that the air was off and the windows were down, Twinkles curled up on the back seat and went to sleep.

"Where's Connor tonight?" I asked as Kay opened her backpack and handed me a soda. I popped the top.

"He had to go watch Ashley receive a humanitarian award."

"Ashely Virginia Randolph got a humanitarian award? I think I believe in unicorns and Death Eaters more than I believe Ashley has a charitable bone in her body."

"She hasn't." Kay pulled out another soda and handed it off. I opened it for her and put it in the other cup holder. "Her daddy gave her a check to give to some arts thing in her name so she could start to be received by society."

"I thought that was why Connor had to learn to fox trot senior year of high school. He was escorting her to her debutante ball, celebrating her coming out in society." I accepted a plastic bowl and put it in my lap.

"I'm ready for that relationship to be over." She pulled out a bag of cheese popcorn and opened it up. "Everyone in the family is ready."

"Is that why your mom doesn't ask for weddings and babies from them?"

"Can you imagine Ashley as a daughter-in-law or as a mother? Mom says a rosary every night that he'll bring home a nice girl. Emphasis on the nice."

"'Nice girl' has a lot of connotations." I held my hand at the rim of the bowl to redirect the wayward popcorn pieces that were pinging out.

"In this case, it's not a sexual scruple. It's about having a bit of empathy. A kind heart. We're all waiting for the magic moment. We know it's coming. Sooner would be better." She tucked the field glasses beside her thigh and rolled the empty bag, then tucked it at her feet.

"What will that look like?" I stuffed a handful of popcorn in my mouth.

"He's waiting. And when what he's waiting for is ready for him," Kay folded her hand over her heart, and spoke with heavy syrup sugaring her words. "He'll move on with his life and live happily ever after. Hand in hand. It will be magical."

"Like the unicorns?"

"Maybe not quite *that* magical."

I licked the salt off my fingers, then wiped them on a napkin. "Ashley is a placeholder?"

"Mutual placeholders. He looks darned handsome in his uniform showing up and shaking hands. But he's got his eye on his prize."

"He already knows who it is?" I leaned forward, wide-eyed. "Who is it?"

Kay blinked at me, picked up her field glasses, and spun to look out the window. "Hey, you know what a unicorn calls their dad?"

I glanced over at her. "What?"

She grinned at me. "Pop Corn."

"Boo. That was really bad, even for you." I threw a couple pieces of popcorn at her. "Cornball."

We sat.

And sat.

And sat some more.

"My ass is falling asleep," I complained. "Maybe we're in the wrong place to be able to see them. I swear to god, they were romping with their ribbons on that hill over there." I pointed.

Kay swung her field glasses left then right. "Maybe we got here too late." She swung right then left then screamed.

The last of the popcorn exploded all over the inside of her car as I jumped at the sudden noise. "What?" I yelled.

"Marley," she said, lifting her hips and rubbing her hand over her bottom. "Whew, I thought I peed myself."

Marley's smoke came into my view before Marley did.

"Hey there," I called, wafting a hand in front of my face, wondering how much smoke I'd need to inhale before I got a second-hand high. I didn't like the sensation of drugs of any kind. And I certainly didn't want to have my imagination rewired while I was searching for unicorns. "I thought I might see you tonight." I reached in my tote and pulled out two bags. "This one's dinner, the other one's breakfast for tomorrow."

"Well, looky here. Thank you. Ain't that nice?" He spit on his fingers, pinched out his joint, and stuck it back in its place behind his ear.

I coughed and swatted my hand back and forth to clear the air. I looked back and saw Twinkles sniffing the air with great enthusiasm. "Stop that," I said, like I had some kind of authority over him.

"We came to see the unicorns humping," Kay said. "Are they out tonight?"

"Sure. Sure. They're over there." He stopped to point. "You ain't gonna be able to spot them from your car, though. I can take you if you want to watch."

I put my hand on the door handle, but Kay swatted her arm out to stop me. "Have you seen any Death Eaters tonight?" she asked.

"Nope. Not hide nor hair of them."

Kay nodded and released my arm. We climbed out of the car and Twinkles decided that he was a tracker like Marley, because they were crouch-stalking side by side. I held the lead because the law told me I had to, and Kay and I walked side by side after them.

Down the hill. Up the hill. Down the hill. I was starting

to get disoriented. And if it weren't for Twinkles's wagging stump of a tail, I'd probably turn around and run back to where we started.

But there! Oh! Down in the valley below!

Kay gasped, spying about thirty men and women in their sequined leotards, with long glossy tails. Some had bits and reins and all of them had horns. Most were prancing about in their hoof boots, doing some version of the minuet to what I'd guess was Medieval chamber music playing over their speakers. Twirling bodies and swirling of ribbons and yup, right there next to the tree, rutting. Lots of rutting.

"Hey, BJ do you know they call a herd of unicorns masturbating?" Kay whispered.

"No, but if it were a herd of cows it would be beef strokin'off." Our head came together as we tried to quiet our snickers.

"No, not a herd," Marley whispered reverently. "I believe they call a group of unicorns a blessing." He slid his headband off and held it to his heart, respectfully.

A blessing it certainly was.

A tear slowly dripped down Marley's craggy cheek. "They're so beautiful."

CHAPTER TWELVE

JOE HAD CLEANED Hooch's in my absence last night. God bless Joe. I needed to do something nice for him. I wondered what he might consider to be nice. I knew what I'd want—a bonus check in my envelope. I sat at my desk, looking over the finances to see if I could swing that. I wanted him happy. He was the Zen master of dishwashing– and he was also a pretty good spy when it came to staying one step ahead of Nicky.

Joe had called it. Nicky had lunched with his ABC buddy, and now a manila envelope, delivered by Deputy Sheriff Wrangles, was propped on my desk. CITATION was stamped across the front in red ink. Mrph. I'd wait until Kay was in so she could decipher the legalese and tell me how much time and money this was going to suck down.

I really needed money. I couldn't depend on Dick to be making bad bets every night. I opened the photos on my phone and looked at the emerald ring. Now here was a dilemma. I'd seen the unicorns and now there were no more reasons to hold back the identity of the family who probably had claim to the locket. *Possibly* had claim to the locket. It had only been identified through the photo I had taken.

But who had the moral high ground?

The locket had been found by emergency personnel; that money would go to the fallen officers' families. If I handed over the possible identification that it belonged to Opal Ruthington and her descendants, then they'd get the locket back. The family might just dig Opal up again, toss it in the box and lower it into the ground. That I found to be sinful.

"Let the police keep the reward," said my good angel.

"Hand it back to the family and let them make the decisions; it is, after all, part of their family's history," said my other good angel.

I looked around for the devil that usually sat on my other shoulder—the one that I had to fight against from time to time.

He cleared his throat. "I don't believe anyone has said anything about the emeralds. It's an odd assumption on your part that the emerald would belong to Opal, as well. After all, we don't know how the locket got from Opal's neck to the alley.

We do know how the emerald got there. Twinkles swallowed it somewhere at some time, and he transported it in his colon. And besides, since it was you who found it, it would be you who could claim the ring if no one else did. And you could use the money."

I looked at my ledger. The devil was right. I really could use the money. And, there was no piece of information that tied the ring to the necklace. My moral dilemma was really only centered around the locket. I'd like to talk it over with Connor, but he'd have to report what I told him. And, of course, he'd know what I was talking about if I offered it up as a hypothetical. I looked down at Twinkles. "What should I do?"

Twinkles raised his brows, gave a full-throated yawn, and closed his eyes.

Twinkles voted to sleep on it. Okay. Maybe I should sleep on it. What could that hurt?

You know what would help me work my way through this dilemma? Having a second source of information. I scrolled forward in my album and looked at Opal's obituary that gave information about her viewing at Greenspoon Funerary Services. I Googled the address. It was a bit of a hike from here, ten blocks. It was four blocks past St. Andrew's Episcopal at the top of Steeple Hill where her services were held.

And look at that: Opal was laid to rest Sunday, the day before I was steaming up Johnson's windows. The first day of the full moon when there was a chance of a unicorn war with the Death Eaters. I thought about Twinkles and his glitter poop after the alley scene. Then my mind went back to the alley scene, when Dick was asking about the locket. I'm pretty sure I saw glitter on that woman's shoes.

Was there glitter on the bottom of Duckie's shoes the night I was doing CPR on her? I texted Dick.

I wasn't sure what that was going to prove to me. If she had glitter it might mean she was walking where the unicorns had been. It could mean that she had found the locket in the graveyard. Of course, even with glitter on her shoes, it didn't mean anything. That locket might never have made itself into Opal's grave. I was really thinking there might be something up with the funeral home. But the jump from up on Steeple Hill to down here in the bottom near the Police Department in the alley near Hooch's... I couldn't make the connection. Felt like there was a connection.

I looked at the time.

Me: **I'm running up the street to Greenspoon Funerary Services to ask some questions. Are you interested in taking a picnic to Marley with me when I get done? I have to pass you on my way down the hill.**

Kay: **I'm beginning to think you have a thing for tie-dye.**

Me: **I just want to get on his good side to see if he'll tell me his dealer—he seems to always have some good stuff.**

Kay: **As if. You hate feeling out of control.**

Me: **Are you calling me a control freak?**

Kay: **Sorta. Yeah, actually :P**

Kay: **That's fine with lunch. I'll stay busy 'til you get here. No rush.**

Me: :))

THE FUNERAL HOME IT WAS. I hadn't been in a funeral home since Memaw died a few years ago. That was my dad's grandmother. She was ninety-nine years young and dancing jigs on St. Patrick's Day, but by April she was sleeping most of the time, and then one day she didn't wake up at all. But that was down on the south side of town. I'd never been to Greenspoon's.

I stood up, and Twinkles pushed to his feet beside me. I considered him, then I considered my outfit of jeans and flip-flops. Probably if I needed to go in to talk to the folks at Greenspoon's, I should do it with a good cover story and no dog.

We walked home. I gave Twinkles a bowl of kibble and changed into a black skirt and heels. I even tugged on a pair of Satan's pantyhose. I pulled a little spandex top on, one that straddled the line of distracting with cleavage and still being considered modest enough for business attire. Though to be honest, it was tilting heavily toward the boob display.

You know, I considered myself a feminist. I thought we should play on an even field. But in covert ops, you had to use all your assets. Instead of playing 007, I was just playing the role of 34DD. (Granted, I needed a touch of padding to get there.)

My phone buzzed.

Dick: **There must be a very good reason you're asking about that. You can tell me tonight. I'll stop by Hooch's after work.**

He didn't answer my question. And he was coming over after work. I wondered if I needed to have another talk about boundaries with him. And oddly, I also thought, Connor might not like Dick trying to expand my boundaries. Huh. That was interesting. I tucked those thoughts away to process another time.

I put a pair of flats in a large purse to change into when I was in the cemetery and left Twinkles asleep in a puddle of sunlight streaming in through my bedroom window.

"HOW DO YOU DO?"

I turned toward the rich baritone voice. My eyes caught on a white shirt. I tilted my head back until I was eye to eye with the man. He was tall and thin and hunched at the shoulders, probably as he tried to curl himself down to a point that people could look him in the eye. I had never seen a guy that tall before, and the word that came to mind was Lurch.

"Hi," I said, my discomfort evident in my voice. It was weirdly quiet, as if the walls had some kind of sound-absorbent materials and I couldn't project my words out beyond my personal space.

He stood and looked at me.

I stood and blinked at him. I rolled my eyes to the right, then the left. I hadn't actually come up with a plan beyond this point.

"May I help you?" he asked.

I stuck out my hand. "Roberta Reid–ling-son." I stammered out.

He shook my hand with the tips of his fingers, which was really weird.

"How may I help you," he tried again.

I was sinking into the thick carpet like quicksand. I lifted one foot, then the other. My mind was racing. I was overwhelmed with the fragrance of carnations. "I've never done this before." I looked around at the warm-colored walls and the serene paintings of nature. "I'm not sure how one goes about arranging things." I frowned, willing my brain to come up with a reasonable scenario for asking about Opal's locket.

He took me under the arm and steered me to the left-hand corridor. "Come. My office is this way. I'll get you a cup of tea. You seem a bit unsteady. Perhaps you would like to sit."

Unsteady would be putting it mildly. Lurch was a little overwhelming. I took advantage of our stroll. I thought I could call myself a cub reporter writing an article about the Greenspoon's service to Jamesburg.

I thought about saying I was writing a paper for a thanatology class. And finally, I decided I needed to plan my mother's funeral. I had no idea if she was alive or dead, in good health or ill. And quite frankly, I couldn't care less. But for the purpose of today, she was on her last breath.

I sat down on a dainty embroidered chair, thinking about how I would act if I were a grieving daughter.

Lurch towered over at the credenza, pouring some hot water in a china cup. "Earl Grey?" he asked.

"Thank you," I said softly, my eyes focused on my hands clenched in my lap. I wished I'd had the forethought to bring a handkerchief.

Lurch placed my cup and saucer on the little table beside me. He took the chair positioned for a conversation. "When you're ready," he said, and sat back with the air of someone who could wait for all eternity if need be.

I gave him a sad little half-smile. "I've never planned a funeral before." I didn't want to outright lie to this guy. And if he had actual work to do, it wouldn't be fair for me to pull him away.

Lurch nodded. "Is this an immediate need? Is there a deceased?"

"Not immediate, no." God this was awkward. The same heebie-jeebies that affected me at Gottlieb's was doing a number on me now. Maybe I had an allergy to blue blood. "I can come back another time." I put my hands on the arms of the chair and began to push myself up.

Lurch fluttered a hand, indicating I was to sit again. "Preparation before a need is always best. My family has been in this business for over a hundred years. I can tell you for certainty failure to prepare will not postpone the inevitable."

Huh. That was bleak.

"Is this service for you?"

"Me?" Oh, hell no! Well, at least I hoped not. I suddenly wanted a mirror to see just how bad I looked. It was a rather hot walk up the hill. But still. I looked like I might be dying?

"A loved one, then."

I bounced forward in the conversation. "What are the steps that are required? What decisions need to be made? I'm taking notes to share with the others." Who the others were, I wasn't quite sure yet. Dick, maybe. Kay for sure. Connor.

"It's a vital role you are playing. Let's begin in the casket room."

Yeah, let's do that.

I took in a deep breath, and it came out a little shaky.

"I am here to support you during this difficult time," he said solicitously, caught me under the elbow, and moved me down the hall to the showroom.

I was freaked out. Lurch was petting the inside of the coffins and talking about how comfortable it was, as if the embalmed body needed satin and a built-in pillow.

"And these in this section are all burping coffins," he said.

"That would explain the price jump," I deadpanned.

"Indeed." He nodded.

Alright, I'd bite. "Why is it important for the coffin to burp?"

"Not to be indelicate, but as a body lays in the coffin, over time a buildup of methane gas occurs. Should one not have a means for allowing the gas to leak out, it could explode."

"Explode?"

"Indeed," he said.

"I've never heard of that. Coffins exploding."

"It's the permeable seal which allows the gas to escape that prevents this."

"But only if you pay extra?"

"No, the escape of gas is required by law. The extra cost here," he gestured with his hand to encompass the display in front of us, "is that these burp."

CHAPTER THIRTEEN

LURCH, led me on a tour of the facilities. He was showing me the various viewing rooms. A slideshow played on a flat screen on the wall. I stopped to watch the photos that seemed to span the last century. And then came to a picture with a tiny slip of a woman lying in her coffin in this very room. I took a step forward. Lurch paused the show. I took another step forward. That was the locket. I was sure of it.

"This is Opal Ruthington," I said.

"You know her?"

"In a way," I said.

"Her family chose the luxury SPZ 9000 for her eternal sleep. Doesn't she look lovely against the pink satin?"

I was almost nose-to-screen now. The locket took up almost the entire chest of the shrunken woman, gleaming against her cream-colored dress. Her head was crowned with a matching cream-colored turban. It was what I imagined the archaeologists would find when they pried open the Egyptian sarcophaguses to fine bejeweled royal mummies inside. "She looks regal," I said. The chain looked too heavy around her scrawny neck. The emerald earrings like the one that Marley found glimmered from earlobes that hung down like curtains beside her jaw. Her hands were folded neatly over her heart and on her pinkie was the ring that Twinkles had pooped out. I was sure of it. *How in the world...?*

"I see she's wearing the family locket. Is that something that is typical?" I asked. "Going to one's rest with the family jewels? Surely you removed these before she was buried."

"Oh, no. No. These jewels were of significance to Miss Ruthington. Of course, she would like to wear them to her just reward."

"At the Pearly Gates."

Lurch nodded.

"To impress St. Peter."

Lurch seemed confused. "Certainly, my more modern clients ask that these are removed for sentimental reasons. They wish to pass them down through the generations. These jewels were placed by Stewart Gottlieb at the family's request. Do you believe that will be something that you will require?"

"Possibly." I turned my head to find a man with heavy brows and a thick square jaw, skulking around the door jamb. He seemed to have his ear cocked and was absorbing everything Lurch was saying. He cast a glare toward me and seemed mighty pissed off–in a respectfully sycophant kind of way, of course.

He pulled his ball cap from his head and held it to his chest. "Mr. Dingleton, if you please."

That's right, Lurch's name was Mr. Dingleton. I practiced it a few times in my head so I didn't accidentally call him Lurch to his face. Then I practiced it a few more times so I wouldn't call him Mr. Dingleberry. Then I decided I should just hedge my bets by keeping my mouth shut.

Dingleton nodded, squeezed my elbow with a slight "stay here" pressure and went to whisper in the hallway.

I put my hand on the side of the burping casket. Leaned over to rest my other hand on my knee and took a few deep breaths.

"GET OUT." Kay bumped her hip into me as we walked side by side back to her car. "There is no such thing as an exploding casket."

"Not if you get one that burps, there isn't. I'm putting that on my high priority list. I don't care if it costs extra."

"You don't even want to be buried. You want to be cremated and you want your ashes sprinkled all over Disneyland."

We climbed into the car.

"I was thirteen when I told you that. I think I've grown out of that phase. Maybe you could just stick my ashes under a tree somewhere and call it a done deal." My stomach was growling. I had the lunch bag perched on my lap. Kay decided she should drive us to the cemetery rather than walk so we had more time to chat with Marley.

"What exactly are we talking to Major Doobie about?" Kay asked, cranking up the air conditioning against the heat of the afternoon sun.

"I don't know that we need him exactly. I'd like to know he has some food. But really, I just wanted to go over and take a look at Opal Ruthington's grave."

"That's not a normal sentence." She put on her blinker and turned right. "Normal people don't say things like that."

"Noted." I couldn't stand it anymore. I reached into the bag and pulled out some fries. They were hot, and I could feel the grains of salt that clung to the grease. I took a deep sniff. This was what I wanted my funeral to smell like. This was so much better than the overbearing scent of carnations.

Kay reached over and grabbed some too, then I rolled the bag shut to keep the heat in. "Do you even know where the grave is?" she asked.

"I was touring the room where Opal was laid out in, I saw her slideshow, and I picked up her flier. It has all the times and places of the different events. Seems we missed out on a bereavement tea given in her honor at the Country Club."

"Shame," Kay said, pulling into a parking spot just to the left of the arch.

"It has a map to her grave."

We unbuckled and climbed out. I was glad Twinkles was back at home and not in danger of finding any unicorn poo. His system was just now getting back to normal.

I started calling, "Marley! Lunchtime. Marleyyyyy!" Then I realized I said the same thing to Twinkles, and that seemed disrespectful.

"You should use a mirror to flash a code. I bet he'd see it from a different state." Kay hopped on one foot while she changed to clog sneakers. She tossed her heels into the front seat and slammed the door.

"He's damned good at that, don't you think?" I asked as we made our way down the path.

"I'd say. As a matter of fact, I might get him to come by my parents' house. I think I dropped the garage key somewhere on the slope. Maybe he'd let me pay him with a hot shower and laundering his things for a finder's fee." Kay pointed at the rainbow colors moving down the hill. "Ta da!"

I handed the bag of food to Kay and pulled out the map, oriented myself, and started heading that way, gesturing to Marley to cut across.

"I can tell you're taking this very seriously," Kay said. "You're wearing pantyhose. I thought that was off the possibility list except for weddings and funerals. Ah," she said. "Got it. She looked over at me. "You must be hating life right about now."

And I was. Who in the fuckity-fuck thought this torture up? I leaned against a tree, hiked up my skirt, and yanked the pantyhose down. With my butt pressed against the trunk for stability, I got them off my feet and put my feet back in my flats. "Whew!" I breathed out as Marley rounded onto our path.

"Lunch?" he asked. I handed him the whole bag. Kay didn't complain. It just meant less cardio when we went to the gym.

Marley opened the bag, stuck his head in, and breathed deeply.

When he came out again with a grin on his face, I had my phone in my hand. "Marley, can I show you a picture?" I asked, turning the image of Opal's locket toward him.

"Purty," he said.

"Have you seen it before?"

"Yup."

"Can you tell me where?"

We all sat down under the tree and Marley ripped open the bag. "Sure. The morning after the officer helped me run off them Death Eaters, I was out surveying. Just lookin' around to see what the D.E.s were up to. I came upon two things." He reached over and tapped my screen. "That necklace and Duckie."

"You know Duckie?" I asked, wide-eyed.

"Sweet old lady, kinda confused, said her name was Duckie and that she was cold. She was crying pretty hard. It nearly broke my heart, so I took her back to my place and tried to get her warm."

"You dressed her in some sweaters and some coats."

"Every last blessed one I had. No matter how many clothes I put on her she kept crying and saying she was cold."

Kay leaned forward. "And then what happened?"

"Finally, I pulled the necklace I found out of my pocket and I give it to her. I said, 'Look how purty, Duckie. Purty necklace for a purty girl.' That got her smiling."

"What did Duckie do next?" I asked, eyes held wide. Small freaking world, wasn't it?

"She walked away." Marley ate a handful of fries. "Haven't seen her since. I've been worried about her, though." His eyes came up and he scanned over the grounds.

"I can tell you that Duckie got sick that night. Kay and I found her and got her some help. Now she's with her family." I waited for him to digest that piece of information and take a bite of the burger. If I was going to keep bringing Marley food, I needed to be thinking in terms of more nutrition and less grease. "Do you remember where you found the necklace? Could you show us after you eat?"

He rolled up the bag and stuck it the hood part of the purple hoodie he was wearing that day. It matched beautifully with his tie-dyed headband. "I'll eat it later. I'm not used to having this much food. My stomach is full." There was no joint behind his ear today; I wondered if he was out.

I wondered if that would be a problem for him and his self-medicating for PTSD. I had no idea how to help him with that one.

"Come on." He swung his arm to gesture the direction we would take. "I wanted to get over that way today anyway. I heard some screaming last night, and I wanted to see what that was about."

"Screaming?" Kay asked.

"Screech owl?" I asked.

"Nope, not a screech owl. Sounded human to me. Female. Sometimes that happens out here. The spirits come up and start moaning and crying in the night. Only reason I thought to look for Duckie and her sobbing was it was daytime. At night, I don't bother. The ghosts settle down by sunrise."

I tipped my head. "You think a ghost was screaming?"

"Not for sure. I was feeling real mellow last night." He reached up to where he usually kept his joint and fingered his bandana. "The sound didn't bother me until I thought about it today. Now that I think on it, it sounded pretty awful."

CHAPTER FOURTEEN

I TRAILED BEHIND MARLEY, and Kay trailed behind me with her hand on my back. I wasn't really in a rush to get down the path. My imagination was dark with possibilities. I pulled my phone from my front pocket, wondering if I should text someone our direction of travel–Dick or maybe Johnson.

My fingers found their way to Connor's quick-dial number.

Kay saw what I was doing, and her hand moved to my shoulder and she steered me while I tapped out the message: **JIC—Kay and I are in the cemetery with Marley, walking east of the entrance arch.**

Connor: **JIC?**

Me: **Just in case.**

Connor: **In case of what? What are you two up to?**

I didn't know *what* we were up to, so I slipped my phone back into my pocket to wait for more information.

We headed up the hill and around an oak. Wait a

minute, I recognized this. I pulled the map out of my pocket and stopped long enough to trace a finger over the map to Opal's grave site. We were heading in that direction. If we kept on, I'd get to go take a look the way I had wanted to.

I was now downwind of Marley. The scent was a fully bloomed bouquet of stale marijuana smoke, and unwashed bodies, with hot meat riding along. I winced and power-walked until I was side by side with Marley.

Marley slowly descended to his crouch—no fast movements for the enemy to see. I came down beside him in a much quicker descent with screaming thigh muscles. Note to self: gym workout, stat. Squats required. I let my knees hit the ground. Kay crouched behind me with her hands on my shoulders, bent low, but not in the dirt. She was wearing her office clothes. We waited.

Marley scanned for a minute, then focused on something. I swiveled my head to see what he'd picked up on, but all I saw were tombstones. Rows and rows of tombstones and trees. His finger traced over the ground and up in front.

"I got me a glimmer," he whispered.

I wondered if it was another earring. Maybe a bracelet this time.

"What do you think it is?" I whispered back.

"Piece of glass."

Piece of glass? How was that interesting enough that I should be grinding my knees into the dirt?

He kept his eye on the distance, then did a slow scan around us and rose to his feet.

Kay reached for my hand and hefted me up. "Gym this afternoon," she said.

Amen to that.

Marley was doing his crouch walk, skulking from tree to tree, shadow to shadow. I wondered if he was having a flashback, whether he'd seen something more than what he was telling us, or whether he was amusing the hell out of himself watching us tiptoeing behind him like the Three Stooges.

Yeah. Shoot. It was the "not telling us everything" one.

I saw the glass now. It was a diamond on a hand. The hand lay in the grass poking out from behind a grave.

"Maybe she's sleeping," Kay said, her voice trembling.

I for one wasn't going to look. Nuh-uh. No way. "Hello? Wake up!" I yelled loudly. I didn't for a second think my yelling was going to work. The hand was grey and waxy, lying palm up. The ring was backwards on her finger and her fingers curled in over it. How Marley saw the glimmer was beyond me. I touched the phone icon on my screen. "Connor?" My voice trembled out as I rounded to the other side of the tree and leaned backward for support. "I think we found a body."

"YOU WEREN'T PURPOSEFULLY LOOKING for a body?" Dick asked. He was standing next to Connor. We were all under the oak, staying out of the coroner's way.

"No," I said for the umpteenth time. "Kay and I brought Marley some lunch."

"Marley, why were you bringing Kay and BJ over here?" Dick asked.

"I wanted to show them the body of the girl who screamed last night."

"You heard her screaming?"

Marley touched the spot where he should have a joint behind his ear. "Yes, sir."

"And what were you doing when you heard the scream?" Dick's pen was poised over a pad of paper.

Marley looked back toward his mausoleum and chewed on the inside of his cheek. His hand reached up and rubbed his cheek and he held it there, obviously thinking hard. When his head came up, he focused right on Dick's eyes. "I was killing her," he said.

Dick paused, then squinted his eyes and asked, "How did you do that?"

"I thunked her over the head with a broken of piece of tombstone."

"She fell to the ground, and you didn't seek help?" Now, one of Dick's eyebrows was quirked up. Yeah, it sounded bogus to me too. Why would Marley say he killed her?

"Well, dead is dead. There ain't much help to be had. And it was dark. Folks don't like to come down here at night except for her. She liked it here. Especially at night." He was pointing over to the stretcher, where they had loaded the body in its black bag. He turned to me. "You know that. You done seen her down here."

I pushed my face forward. "I saw who?"

"The girl with the glass ring. You and Kay was talking to her when your dog was licking at the unicorn poop. You shouldn't let him eat that stuff. Bet it gave him a terrible bellyache."

"You saw us talking to someone?"

"Yeah, the purty blond girl."

I reached out a hand and grasped at Kay. Kay grasped back. My gaze slowly moved between Connor and Dick and back to Connor. "Felicia?"

Connor's face turned red.

Dick cleared his voice. "We aren't able to identify a body without going through procedures. It's against regulation."

"It appears to be Felicia?" I tried again.

Both men nodded. I sank down until my butt hit the ground. Whomp. Felicia. *Felicia?* Felicia. Nope, my brain wouldn't process it. Connor rolled Kay into his shoulder—she was bawling big time. Marley just stood there, looking mellow.

Dick turned to Marley. "Why did you kill her?"

Marley shrugged.

"Do you know her personally?"

"Nope. Just seen her around from time to time. I bonked her on the head and now she's dead. Guess I need to go to jail." Marley turned around and put his hands behind his back, ready for the cuffs.

I shook my head back and forth, not able to process what was going on. None of it made sense to me.

If everything would stop for a nanosecond my brain could catch up, and I could reason my way through this.

Felicia was dead.

Dead by a blow to the head from mellow Marley. No, that didn't add up. And yet, there was the coroner's assistant, sliding the body, zipped up in a black bag, into their truck. Here was Officer Connor Fitzgerald cuffing Marley and reading him his rights.

And yes, now that I think back, that hand with its turquoise nail polish and big-ass diamond ring looked exactly the way Felicia's had the last time I saw her, which was last night, when I left her to lock up Hooch's so Kay and I could eat cheesy popcorn and watch the unicorns frolicking in the meadow.

If Marley had killed Felicia, he could just as easily have killed us.

CHAPTER FIFTEEN

I SAT on the orange plastic chair in the visitor's room at the jail with thick plastic glass on one side and a well-used black phone receiver waiting to be picked up. Inmates began to take their seats in the cubicles, all in a straight line.

I didn't know why I was there. Yes, there was Felicia's murder, and Marley might just have the information that was needed to solve it. But to be honest, I felt a kinship to Marley ever since he rapped on Johnson's window and told us that there was about to be an epic war that he needed to stop. No, I think it was when he saluted and went off to do recon that I felt attached to Marley.

Maybe it was because he served our country and then was punished for it once he got back.

When I was younger, my father told me about my Uncle Paul, who had gone off to war. Back then, in the sixties, no one wanted to truly do it. There was a draft, and he fit Uncle Sam's bill. Dad told me that he came back a little messed up–seeing war when he closed his eyes.

I don't remember my Uncle Paul, although Dad tells me

that he used to toss me up in the air as high as he could in hopes that I'd fly like the angels. I remember him giving me a shiny quarter whenever he stopped by.

Uncle Paul disappeared, and my dad never stopped looking for him. Maybe that's why this stranger had so much meaning for me. Here was a soldier that I could maybe help when I couldn't help my dad and Uncle Paul.

I looked around. It was a small room with a camera in each corner and a partition down the middle. On one side the inmates sat behind the thick glass, and on the other side sat the visitors. Some sniffled into the phone, others shared intimate talk, but me, I just waited patiently for Marley to show up.

The glass was scratched up and scarred, and the tabletop dented. The paint had been rubbed and scratched off parts of the legs. It looked like it had seen its fair share of visitations. I wondered how many innocent people had sat in those chairs behind that glass, begging their loved ones to believe in them.

I wondered how many innocent people had sat at this table deciding that they didn't have it in them to fight for their freedom. But Marley hadn't been scooped up in a mistake—he had confessed at the scene.

Weird. I didn't buy it.

Marley shuffled in wearing an orange jumpsuit, white socks, and shower shoes. He was handcuffed. He was also clean. His hair was just past his shoulders and stood out in a big poofy cloud of waves, without the constraint of a ponytail holder or a bandana. The guard pointed at the cameras and went out. I heard the lock being thrown on the door, and I have to admit, it was alarming. And a little claustrophobic.

Marley sat down and shoved his hair out of his eyes the best he could with his cuffed hands. "Nice to see you, BJ."

I gave him a *don't hand me that shit* look. He looked at his feet.

"Why is your hair in your face?" I asked.

"My rubber band snapped. And they won't let me have the bandana in here."

"I'm sorry. I'll ask the guard if I can give you my hair elastic." I leaned forward. "Without any crap, Marley, why did you want to come to jail?"

"I got me a terrible toothache, and they got dentists on hand."

"You said you murdered someone."

"I said I bonked her on the head, too. I doubt that's what killed her. It's hard to kill someone with a single bonk on the head."

"Unless you know where to hit them."

"Yep."

"And they could make the case that, with your time in Vietnam, you have that skillset."

"Damned."

"Uh-huh." I considered him for a moment. "We need to get you out and find out what really happened."

Marley sat there with a deep frown.

"How did she really die? What do you know about it? You said you heard a scream."

"As to the dying stuff? I have no idea—I discovered her same time you did."

"But you knew who it was."

"Recognized her hand - blue nails and fake ring."

"Her ring was fake?" *What?* Her fiancé was a jeweler, for heaven sake.

"Glass don't shimmer the same way as a diamond do. Got a different glint."

Hmm, I wasn't sure if that was important or not. It did up the picture of Stewart as a colossal creep that I had in my head, though. I could see him doing that. Lying about the ring. Stewart... I should go pay him a visit.

"You heard a scream. How confident are you that it was Felicia screaming?"

"Before she screamed, I heard her talking. It was her voice, and his."

"His?" This was like playing Mother, May I, and I had to get permission to take each step forward toward my intended goal. My goal? Get Marley out of here and find him a dentist. Maybe put the police on the trail of the murderer so the bad guy wasn't hanging out in our city, walking around freely, maybe killing again.

"It was the tree guy." And he tapped his head.

I didn't know what that could mean. "Tree guy?"

"Yup."

"Anything more than tree guy?"

"Sure, they were up in the cemetery all the time, walking around, talking. They were always up there after a funeral to look at the new grave and talk about it."

"Always new graves?"

"Well, there ain't a lot of new funerals here. Grounds are all sold off. So those with family plots can be buried. All them families deal with Greenspoon's."

"Felicia—well, the dead woman—came to see all of the graves after Greenspoon put a body in that grave?"

Holy moly. I just had a terrible thought. If that was actually Felicia, she would, as Stewart's fiancée, have access to his obituary books. He might tell her over dinner when he was going to fancy up a dead client. What if she was engaged to Stewart for this data alone? She would know what graves to rob. Could Felicia do such a thing for the money? For her mom? Hmm. I might be able to convince myself to rob a grave to save my dad. No real harm done, right? Yeah, actually, I bet that if I needed money to save Dad and I had *this* way to do it? I'd do it, too. "Would you recognize the tree guy if you saw him again?"

"He wore a hat. I didn't never see his face."

"What kind of hat? Like a baseball cap?"

"Yep. Baseball cap–I don't think I could recognize him in person. His voice, though, that I could recognize." He nodded. "Yep. I'd know the voice." He rubbed his wrist under one of the cuffs. "I think I made a big mistake telling them I done did it. The toothache must have poisoned my brain."

"I'm sure the truth will come out." I reached out and put my hand on the glass. "In the meantime, I wanted your permission to go by your mausoleum and get any of your bedding and clothes and get them washed for you so when you get home, everything is nice and fresh."

Marley nodded and I took that as permission granted. He was looking at his thumbnail where the dirt had rubbed so deep into his skin, I doubted he'd ever be really clean again. "I done messed up."

"It might take some time to figure this out, but I'm sure justice will prevail. I just want you to be honest and only speak the truth from here on. If you need a dentist, I can help you get that–no need to lie for dental care."

"Okay," Marley said, and it was the saddest two syllables I think I'd ever heard.

I STILL HADN'T GOTTEN any confirmation back from anyone that the dead woman was for sure Felicia, and I preferred to spend my time waiting in denial. Denial didn't work very well when you sit still. Action was required. Distraction was probably the better word. So off I went with a couple oversized garbage bags to load up Marley's things and take them back to my apartment to get them clean.

Walking into someone's camp, their home, felt intrusive. But he had given me permission, I reminded myself. I could have guessed that what little Marley had was neatly stacked and organized. I had filled up two bags and was on my third when I came across a new-looking baseball cap sitting upside down on a perfectly folded blanket pile. I reached for the bill to drag it over and found it was heavy.

Something was inside.

As I pulled the cap toward the opening, and daylight, I spotted a necklace. It was a doozy of a necklace, too. There were six strands of graduated pearls that went from choker-length to mid-chest-length strands. They were gathered up in the center with the largest ruby I had ever seen. Maybe it wasn't a ruby; maybe this was a garnet or something. I wasn't great when it comes to gemstones, since I disliked jewelry as a whole. All around the outside of the center stone were fire opals.

Now those I recognized. They were interspersed with little diamonds. I rocked back on my heels. "Holy cow, this must be worth a freaking fortune," I said out loud.

Now, despite what people might think, finders, keepers wasn't a legal thing. And possession is nine-tenths of the law, but mrph, that's not really right either. If you find something of value, you have to give it to the police. It has to be processed properly. Marley had told Kay and I that he had found it, and I had believed him.

I still believed him.

But I had also thought it was a piece of Target jewelry, the kind you can get for $19.99 to wear with a pair of jeans and a cute top. I had no idea that it was a treasure. Marley had also said he was sure that someone would come back looking for this necklace, and he would return it to them. He meant to do the right thing. I believed that, too.

Why would someone be wandering in the graveyard wearing a necklace like this? This was something you might wear to meet the queen, or maybe to an inauguration ball.

I looked at the necklace and wondered what would happen if I pawned it and gave the money to Marley to hire a real lawyer. Maybe even someone from Kay's office. The idea came and the idea went.

I couldn't leave a necklace of this value sitting out here.

I couldn't take it with me.

Really, my only choice was to call the police and hand it over to them. If I mentioned Marley had found it, would that get him in bigger trouble? If I didn't mention Marley, would they ask me where I found it? Would that get me in trouble? I was already in trouble enough with the ABC crapola. Undeserved trouble, but trouble all the same.

Shit.

I didn't know what to do and who to ask, because asking anyone would get them involved. And anyone who got anywhere near this thing would sink deep and stay stuck.

I sat outside of the mausoleum with my back against the marble blocks, the necklace in my lap.

Shit, I thought again, then pulled out my phone and called Connor.

CHAPTER SIXTEEN

I WAS in the shower when the *catchunk, catchink, catchunk* dragged me away from my thoughts. It was my second shower of the day. One this morning before I went to the jail, and this one, now that I was home from the Marley's mausoleum. This wasn't a get-clean shower; it was a think-things-through shower. I always had my best ideas as the hot water sluiced over my hair. It revved my brain.

Connor had confirmed that it was Felicia's body we'd found. But she had been strangled, not bludgeoned. Yes, the DA was still moving forward with a case against Marley, even though his confession said nothing about strangulation. Connor put the necklace into an evidence bag and thought that that was another nail in Marley's coffin, so to speak. Things weren't looking good for him.

"Don't you think it's fishy? It serves no one to put the wrong guy behind bars," I'd challenged him.

"Agreed. Dick's been doing interviews trying to find any enemies, any personal issues, and it seems straightforward.

Felicia lead a clean life, was engaged to a member of old Jamesburg society; Marley is a homeless addict."

"Self-medicating," I objected.

Connor had frowned.

Catchunk. Catchink.

I reached for a towel and wrapped myself in it as I made my way to the washer. *What if Felicia wasn't as clean as she appears to be, Connor?*

The guy in the cemetery every time there was a service —he could have been an accomplice. She'd need an accomplice to get the coffin open. My mind went to that square-jawed guy with the heavy eyebrows at the funeral parlor. He looked like he could wear a baseball cap and get up to no good. I opened the door on the washer to stop the spin cycle and fished my hand around inside. My fingers wrapped around a piece of metal, and I pulled it out.

I held it in the flat of my hand. I had no idea what it was that I was looking at. About the diameter of a pencil. It looked a little like an Adam's wrench or corkscrew without the threading. I laid it on my kitchen floor and took a picture of it, then put it through a Google image search. Seconds later, I knew. It was a coffin key. And with another Google search, I learned that after a viewing, the coffin is locked and the key hole plugged before it is lowered into the ground. If you were going to rob a coffin, you'd need a key, like this one, to get it open. Oh, Marley! Why would you have a coffin key in your camp?

I went to get dressed, then moved the wet things to the dryer. I opened the next bag to put in the wash. Kneeling on the floor, I gave each piece a little shake and felt the pockets to make sure I wasn't putting anything else in my machine that didn't belong there.

Maybe I was wrong about Marley.

Maybe he was in cahoots with Felicia, if indeed Felicia was up to something nefarious...But then why would Marley get Johnson to stop the Death Eaters if that was the case?

Marley had told us the Death Eaters came when there was fresh meat to be had, when the grass could be rolled away and the earth was still easily dug. So confusing. I put the washer on the sanitize cycle and pressed the start button. I kicked the third bag to the corner to deal with later. I needed to head back to the funeral parlor. I needed a picture of the guy who was eavesdropping in the doorway, the one with the angry eyes.

I SHOWED up at Greenspoon's without an alibi. I'd already used the "a loved one is in hospice care" line and truth be told, I didn't want to use it again. I thought it might be tempting fate. I was standing outside the front door on the walk, trying to conjure a good excuse to find the worker, when I saw him climb out of a truck in the parking lot. I slid behind a tree. Standing in the shadows, I took photos of him as he came up the walk. He removed his cap, ran his fingers through his hair, and put the cap back on his head, pulling the bill low over his eyes.

After a few more steps, he turned away from me and made his way down the sidewalk and around the corner. I waited until he was out of view then I followed after him. Dingleton—Lurch—was conferring with him beside the hearse.

"We have a pickup at the medical examiner's office. Felicia Mulvane. Here's the paperwork," Lurch said.

I started recording them.

"Did you finish up the Tyler burial? Is it ready for visitors?" Lurch asked.

"Yes, sir. The coffin is covered, the headstone properly placed, and I arranged the flowers the way you asked. Do I need to go up and mark the plot in the Gottlieb family section?"

"No, that won't be necessary. The Mulvane family will be handling her funeral arrangements. Seems as if they already had arrangements in place for the mother, a plot and all. A shame that it will be used for the daughter. A tragedy, really. They're only putting out for the HNF770 with the acetate lining." Disdain dripped from his voice. "She'll be placed in the Dignity Cemetery, where the plot was previously purchased. They're going low-budget, so the niceties will be dispensed with."

"Yes, sir."

And he was gone.

I spooled back to the other side of the building again. Did I need any more information? I didn't think so. I had pictures and I had voices. Now I needed to figure out whether Marley recognized either man as the one who was in the graveyard with Felicia.

As I climbed back in my car, I looked at the time. The day had flown by. That's what happened when your schedule meant you sleep from sunrise until noon. *If* you can sleep. Lately, sleep had been evading me.

I powered down the road toward Hooch's. I was going to be on my own again, taking care of the bar, now that Felicia was dead. Wasn't that a selfish tack for my brain to take?

Speaking of weird tacks, I found myself pulling up in front of Gottlieb Family Jewelers. I was surprised to find it open for business. And just as surprised to find myself shifting into park.

Well, might as well make the most of it. I went inside. Stewart was walking toward the door with his keys in his hands. He backed up as I pushed the door open.

"Stewart, Felicia. I don't know what to say. Are you okay?"

He frowned at me. There was an uncomfortable pause.

"It's five o'clock," he said.

"Right." Not what I expected from a bereaved fiancé. "I was wondering about the arrangements for Felicia's funeral. Are you handling them?"

"No," he said.

And that's when my mouth started working faster than my brain. "You know, Felicia was very much concerned about animals. The rescue society was a big deal to her. As a matter of fact, she suggested to me a way that I could help spread the word through having some of my friends pose for a calendar with rescue puppies. But I'm sure you know this."

He stared at me blankly.

"I know that it's part of what you do to bury people with their significant jewelry. But, and please excuse me for overstepping, I just thought that it would be a lovely gesture if you were to use her engagement ring to support this cause rather than let it go in the ground with her. I'm sure she would prefer it."

"That ring is of little to no value," he said. "As she knew well."

My eyebrows went up.

"It is a glass replica of the ring she would receive after we were married."

I shook my head, not following. But I did light on the fact that Marley was right—the ring was glass, not diamond.

Stewart heaved a sigh. "I learned my lesson from my father. He gave an exquisite ring to my half—" he paused with a choking sound—"brother's mother after my own dear mother departed this world. The woman accepted the ring, but then refused to marry him."

"And he didn't try to get it back?"

"And expose our family to ridicule? Preposterous. Now if you'll excuse me, a friend is waiting to console me with drinks at the club."

Holy moly.

I gave him a weak smile. "Please let me know if there is anything I can do."

"As a matter of fact, you can. I would prefer that Felicia's name was never associated with *Hooch's*." Contempt painted from his voice. "Keep any monies she might have earned and destroy any of her paperwork. She merely took the job there to make a point to me. The point was taken in due course. And Felicia was taken care of."

A shiver ran from the nape of my neck down to my heels. I nodded and burst out the door, scrambled over to my Mini Cooper, and jumped in. Stewart was right behind me. I tapped my phone to stop the video that had been taken in my pocket.

Yes, I knew that there were laws in Virginia against recording someone's voice without their permission. But hey, it wasn't my fault if my phone happened to record our conversation while in my pocket, and I found it later. Right?

I lifted the lens up and took several pictures of Stewart as he got in his car. I would ask Marley about Stewart too. What could he mean by "Felicia was taken care of?"

CHAPTER SEVENTEEN

I WAS at odds with myself. I wasn't quite sure what to do. Kay had offered to meet me at the gym, and we could grab a sandwich after, but that time had come and gone. In her last text, she said she was going to go home and binge Netflix unless I needed her, in which case I should call. I wouldn't call. I wasn't going to take advantage of our friendship.

Connor said the same. He had a shift to work, but he'd be happy to stop in and check on me. I didn't want to be that person–needy. Besides, I had Joe in the back, softly singing Hungarian lullabies.

Two guys sat in a booth with beers. A couple was in the corner with a yellow legal pad between them, making some plan or another. She drank a Zinfandel, and he went for the Badge Bunny Booze. I settled a platter of nachos in front of some boys in blue. They had the badges, but they also had greying hair and Dunlop disease. That's when the belly done lopped over their tool belt. And that just wasn't my thang. Their beers were nearly drained; they'd need another round soon.

I parked behind the counter and scrolled through the information I had gathered: pictures of Lurch and the scowler at the funeral parlor; pictures of Stewart getting into his car to go have drinks at the club; the ruby necklace, the locket, the earring.

I hadn't told anyone that I thought I knew who the jewels belonged to. I still had a big dose of "if the family thought they were okay to go into the ground, then the family doesn't deserve them back" mentality, and that was now counterweighted with "I think this is why Felicia is dead."

Felicia was dead. It still sounded weird in my head. I needed to tell someone about the jewels. And I would. But first, I wanted to see Marley and ask if he recognized any of these men.

People began to file into the bar. Chairs filled. The noise level picked up. For a Friday night, things were buzzing in the bar. Not so much that I couldn't handle it. Enough though that I would be able to pay the light bill.

I needed to work on my list of cops for the puppy calendar—a tribute to Felicia. I should finish my list and figure out how I'd pitch the project.

Pitching in person was going to be the way to go. It was easy to say no to a letter; it was so much harder to say no to a direct appeal. Stroke their ego, lay it on heavy about helping the greater good. I pulled out a pad and pen and wrote Johnson, Dick, Peter, Willy, Woody... Then I smiled thinking it sounded like a list of gifted tallywackers.

Marley had said that there weren't many people who were buried at St. Clemmons anymore–just the old families.

I wondered if Evelyn Chiles was among the obits pictures I had taken. I had six, and Marley said she was buried around Veterans' Day. I leaned onto my elbows and scrolled through my photos.

Fifth one back. Yep. Here she was.

I spread the screen so I could read it and noticed for the very first time that under the obituary, in precise up-and-down strokes, there was a list of jewels.

Pearl and ruby necklace circa 1890. Present value $72,600. Diamond ring, 1948, Present value $39,000. Drop natural pearl earring with diamond bows 1928, present value $55,000. I did some quick mental math. $166,600.00.

That wasn't a coffin. That was a treasure chest.

I moved forward to find Opal's obituary. *Bejeweled locket circa 1841, present value $29,500.00. Emerald and diamond cocktail ring and earring set circa 1969, present vale $41,800.* Hers was worth less, only $71,300.

But if you could get away with it scot-free and no one was reporting it stolen, there were no police on your tail and no chance of the jewels showing up on a police list, then you wouldn't need to fence them. You could go to a legitimate auction house or estate jeweler and sell them for their full market price. It was brilliant.

I moved through each obituary, taking notes. On the six obituaries I had photographed, all were buried in St. Clemmons. And the take would be well over a million dollars.

Who had access to them?

Stewart, the people from Greenspoon's, the groundskeeper at the cemetery. Mmm, no. I really didn't think it would be them. They wouldn't need to come back. They'd just needed to pop the top before they covered it over.

It could be Marley... but that didn't ring true.

Felicia? Yeah, that felt right. Felicia died because Felicia was up to no good. Well–probably a lot of good in her own mind. She was Robin Hood, one could argue, stealing from the dead to give to the living. In this case, get her mom the medical help she needed.

Felicia? Probably. But again, this was just my internal gyroscope, and I had no proof of anything.

I thought back to the funeral home and the heavy scent of flowers that filled the place. Marley said the Death Eaters came out the day after the funeral, never the day of.

The very top obituary in the book, the newest, listed the date for the funeral service. And her jewels were worth over $200,000.

If what I thought was happening was actually what was happening, then the bad guys (or girls) were about to cash in on a major payday.

CHAPTER EIGHTEEN

IN THE MATH equation of bed plus exhaustion equals snooze, my current state didn't add up.

I kicked my legs to untangle them from my sheets. I'd been floundering around, fish-like, unable to get my mind to shut up long enough that I could dive into the theta waves of deep sleep.

I drifted off enough to have some uncomfortable nightmares and now I was giving up. I reached for my phone. Connor, I thought, but nope. He was helping his dad today. Kay, I thought. Nope, she was picking up Terrance at the airport. Johnson? I tapped on the contact number and sent him a quick text.

Me: **Are you up?**

Johnson: **Every time you text. You have that effect on me.**

Well, my mind wasn't really going there, but I have to admit, picturing Johnson in his ready position sent a little zippity to my doo-dah. I shook my head. Eyes on the prize.

Okay, not that prize. The other one—getting Marley out of jail and to a dentist.

Me: **Official police business.**

Johnson: **Okay. I'm just going to bed. Can it wait until I'm functioning in official police capacity?**

Me: **In your uniform.**

Johnson: **Ready, willing and able.**

Me: **Tease.**

Okay, I'd have to wait to lay this out for him and see what he thought. So far it was just puzzle pieces, and none of the colors and shapes seemed to fit together. I needed to talk to Marley some more.

I watched the coffee slowly dripping into the carafe. Sloooowly. I sighed, pushed off the counter, and went to throw another load of Marley's things into the wash. I decided to run by the hardware store to get him some plastic bins with stay-shut tabs to put his things in, and maybe pick up a sleeping bag and new pillow while I was at it.

The washer was almost full when I reached in the bag and pulled out the navy-blue ball cap that had held the ruby necklace. This time it was upright, and I was looking at the logo on the front. A tree. Didn't Marley call that the guy who hung out in the cemetery "tree man?" Was it because he wore this hat?

I took a picture of the logo and loaded it into Internet image search, which almost never let me down. The Internet let me down. Mrph. It was a free graphic that was used by a shit-ton of businesses. Yes, that was the actual number. Shit-freaking-ton. And when I tried to add Virginia it didn't narrow the parameters. I tried just Jamesburg Virginia and got the same way-too-long list. Boo.

And again, I was jumping to conclusions. I had read a lot of police procedurals, and I knew this hat was probably a red herring. What were the facts? The jewels I'd seen corresponded with the information in Stewart's book.

My coffee was done perking. Marley was in jail for a crime that I was pretty sure he didn't commit. Twinkles needed to pee. Felicia was dead.

I put coffee in a to-go cup. I decided my pajamas looked enough like exercise clothes that I didn't need to change. I slipped on my tennis shoes, tied up the laces, snapped the lead onto Twinkles's collar, and off we went. Twinkles was almost back to his natural color in the number two department, and there was only a tiny sprinkle of glitter. I didn't think I needed to worry about him anymore. He was resilient. I did need to worry about Marley.

I took Twinkles home and made quick work of getting myself together. "You have to wait here. I won't be long," I told Twinkles as I shoved my phone in my back pocket and put the hat in a brown paper bag.

"YOU CAME to see me again. I'm thinking you like me." Marley smiled, but his eyes were dim—and not in the "I'm feeling no pain thanks to my weed" way, more of a "I'm struggling to keep it together" way.

"I do like you." I opened up the bag that the guards had thoroughly examined before I came in. "I wanted to show you something. Do you remember that you said I could wash your things for you?"

"Yup."

"I found this hat." I put it on the table. "I also found the necklace."

He blinked.

"I gave the necklace to Officer Fitzgerald. He has it at Headquarters. He's going to try to find the owner for you."

"That's good," Marley said.

"The necklace was in the hat. Is there a reason?"

"I found them together."

"Ah." I wasn't sure about Marley's brain health. I didn't want to plant any false memories. I had to be careful how I phrased things. "Have you ever seen this hat before you found it?"

"Yep. It belonged to the tree guy who talked to your friend."

"Felicia?"

"Felicia."

"And you found it around what time of year?"

"Veterans' Day."

That's what he'd said before. "Can you describe the tree man?"

"He was tall."

I waited.

"He wore a belt with a shiny buckle."

I waited.

"He has a voice like a truck."

"That you'd recognize?"

"Yep."

I scrolled through my phone and showed him a picture of Lurch, the other funeral guy, and Stewart. Marley identified each of them as being around the burials, but neither of them was the tree man. I wasn't sure the tree man was important here.

"When the Death Eaters were around, did you hear them talk?"

"Yep, but the sound of the dog growling was pretty loud."

"How many Death Eaters do you think there were?" I'd asked him before and he'd said he thought they were a breeding pair, but I wanted to see if that still held up.

"Three," he said without even thinking. "Two males and a female."

Okay, that was new. "Anything else you can tell me?"

"My tooth hurts and the dentist isn't scheduled to come until next month."

MY TRIP TO see Marley wasn't as productive as I'd hoped. I was back in my car feeling... I guess 'discombobulated' might be the appropriate word. I found myself driving toward the cemetery. I walked the hills, thinking for such a seemingly peaceful spot, a lot of shit sure did happen out here. And, ironically, I stepped over a pile of glitter poop.

I stopped by Evelyn Chiles's grave. Then I stopped by Opal's. "Opal," I said. "I hope you're okay. Sorry someone took your necklace if you wanted to keep it. I can tell you that it was a relief to an old lady who was very upset. Now Connor is going to talk to your family to see if they can identify it. See if he can't get it back to them. It's not the same thing as having it down there, but it's better than having it stolen and sold. Right?"

I heard a car motoring down the street at a distance.

"Look, it's just you and me chatting here. Not that I'm encouraging you to haunt me or anything. As a matter of fact, I'd be really appreciative if you didn't haunt me. But do you have any information? Is there anything at all you could tell me?"

I sat and waited.

I looked around.

I waited some more.

I got up and brushed the grass off my butt and said, "Okay, I'm headed over to Drusilla Washington's grave. If you think of anything..." I strolled off over the hill, around the tree, to the other side of the statue and found the new grave with the shiny marble headstone and the fresh flowers just starting to wilt. Everything looked the way it should. The grass lined up nicely in the corners. The headstone was plumb. "Still wearing your jewels? Everything okay down there?"

That's when the wind kicked up. And I mean big-time. It blew my hair into my face. I had to turn one-eighty so I could see. I pulled an elastic band off my wrist and wrestled the strands together. One of the flower displays, the one with the heart that said "Mother," cartwheeled off, rolling over the wreath part and hopping over the tripod of legs part. I looked at Drusilla's grave. "Don't worry, I'll get it for you." And I started chasing after it. *Drusilla—who gives a name like that to their child?*

It wasn't until the wreath wedged itself behind a building that I was able to catch hold of it. I pressed my back against the ancient stone wall and caught my breath. Well, good, I could check the gym off my list of things to do that day. I had worked up a good sweat and my quota for an elevated heart rate.

The little building I leaned against had dusty windows. I cupped my hands around my eyes and looked in. This must be the groundskeeper's storage. I saw mowers and landscaping paraphernalia–weed eaters, grass seed, and pesticides. Nothing very interesting.

"Opal, was that you blowing this wreath over here? Was

there something you wanted me to see?" Yeah, I knew I sounded slightly insane, but the wind had kicked up out of nowhere. And as soon as I got here, it stopped. Weird. Maybe eerie was a better word. I stuck my arm through the hole in the wreath and turned to head back to put it in place when I heard a truck chug to a stop. I peeked around the corner of the building. A dualie with a trailer had pulled up on the dirt service road. Two men climbed out of the cab. They were pretty far away; I couldn't make them out very well.

I put the wreath by the door and snuck around to the other side of the building. Stooping low, à la Marley, I tiptoe-ran from the house to the wooded area. I jogged deeper into the trees until I knew I couldn't be seen, then cut over to bring myself parallel to the truck. On my hands and knees, I crawled toward the utility road. Then I was on my belly. I was still far away. The men weren't there. Hmm.

Using my phone, I took a picture of the truck, then opened my gallery and spread my fingers on the screen until I could see quite clearly the logo was the same as the one on the hat I had shown Marley. Nothing nefarious about that; this was just some maintenance crew that worked to keep things spiffy. Still, it would be good to get the company's name. I texted the photo to Kay, Connor, Dick, and Johnson. The group text read:

Have any of you ever seen this logo before? It may have to do with the cemetery upkeep, but Marley didn't know. Might be a friend of Felicia's???

The two men were working at the trailer, fussing with the ramp. A minute later, an engine revved. Growled, actually. I backed into the woods, then cut further down until I was behind the trailer and came back over. From here, I could see the head of one man where he sat in the cab of a small digger. He drove it down the trailer ramp.

As it came into full view, I gasped. It was painted to look like a dog. The headlights were the eyes, and the jaw parts were painted like jaws. This was what Marley saw when the Death Eaters were in the graves. These must be the Death Eaters!

The guy killed the engine, and while I couldn't see either of their faces, I could hear them talking about the Yankees baseball game. I took a video, then sent a follow-up text.

I took this at St. Clemmons. Heading back now. I need to ask Marley if he recognizes either of these voices. He thinks that Felicia's real killer was a guy she hangs out with who wears this logo on his hat. Maybe Marley'll recognize the men's voices.

I flipped back to my camera when suddenly I was flung full-force into the ground. The velocity pushed all the air from my body. I was pinned under an enormous weight.

"Well, well, well, look what we've got here. Hey, Chris, come see what I found."

I was trapped. I couldn't see who was on top of me. I couldn't see Chris as he approached except for his muddy work boots. He wrenched my phone out of my hand and scrolled through my pictures and video. "Looks like we've got ourselves a Nancy Drew wannabe." He pitched my phone down beside me and crushed it with his heel, cracking the screen.

"Go get some zip ties from the cab. We need to truss her up."

CHAPTER NINETEEN

WELL, here's an unexpected twist. Okay, a couple of unexpected twists. My arm! Ouch!

The guy had wrenched me to my feet. As I stood, I got a look at his face. Frank *freaking* Mason, the half-brother, the canoodling soon-to-be (well, would-have-been, was more accurate) half-brother-in-law of Felicia's.

Did I describe him as six-foot-heaven? That suddenly changed to six-foot-oh-hell-no! He was every bit as ablebodied as I wished he wasn't, I thought as I wriggled around trying to find my way out of his grip. I stopped, mid-wriggle. I'd just exhaust and probably hurt myself.

His level of physical prowess meant that I needed to engage what I hoped was superior thinking power.

Okay...

Hmm, maybe my thinker was turned off for the moment; I was getting nothing.

There was no one who could hear me scream. That was about the extent of the rumble in my gray matter.

Then a couple other thoughts bubbled up: He'd ground

my phone into dust. And I wasn't dressed for this. I really needed some kind of superhero suit with integrated weaponry. My loudest thought was I needed to pee. Bad.

Yup, those bad-*boy* vibes he'd radiated at the bar were really bad-*guy* vibes. I needed to check the controls on my danger meter; the reading was too weak.

Frank shoved his hand on my head, forcing me to look at the ground as the two men conferred above me.

"What the hell is she doing out here crawling around in the trees?"

"She's spying."

"You moron," the other guy said. "We're dressed to look like we belong here. If you hadn't grabbed her, we could have just kept on keeping on. Now we can't do that, now can we?"

"Watch who you're calling moron. She was taking a video of us, lying on her stomach in the woods. Do you really think that she just thought we were out here doing grounds work?"

"Why were you out here?" the other man demanded.

"I was bird-watching," I said. Hey, that wasn't half bad.

"You were taping us," Frank countered with a squeeze and a shake.

That's going to leave a bruise.

"You were in the tape, but only because there was a blue-bearded eastern finch behind you. They're very rare. Almost unheard of." Well I'd never heard of one before. "I had been following it, waiting for it to settle so I could take video and show my ornithology friends."

"What the hell is an ornithology friend?" Frank asked.

"My friends who like to bird-watch and share rare birds they spot."

"Oops," Frank said.

Yeah, that was putting it a bit mildly. "Look, no harm, no foul." And then my nerves go the best of me, and I started laughing. Hard. "See what I did there?" I sputtered. "No harm, no foul? No harm, no fowl? *Fowl?*" I glanced up between the two men's faces. My sense of humor was lost on them. I sobered. "Look, I'm sorry I spooked you. It must have been weird to find a chick crawling around in the woods, and then seeing she was taking a video, and thinking the she was focused on videoing you." And then I went straight for the guy's ego. "Though, I'm sure you get that a lot. Women, that is, following you around, trying to get video of you. Handsome as you are. All tall and muscular..."

Frank contemplated for a moment, his head tipped to the side, a slight nod of affirmation. Hope bubbled up inside me. Maybe I *could* outthink them.

"But yeah," I finished. "I really was focused on the blue beard. I understand that you'd want to find out what I was up to. And now you know. You can let go of my arm now."

He let go of my arm.

It lasted a microsecond. Not long enough for me to push the go button and race out of his reach, though I'm sure the adrenaline juicing my body would let me run like a gazelle, or maybe even a freaking unicorn.

As Frank's hand left my left arm, the other guy grabbed my right. "She's going to tell this story around. She's seen our faces. We're already walking thin ice because Felicia got cold feet."

"Shit man, now you said Felicia. Now we can't let her go," Frank said, tossing his hands in the air.

"I'm sorry, did you say something? I was in la-la land for a second," I said, hoping it might work.

It didn't work.

"We're going to have to take care of her. If we do it now,

it'll leave less mess. If we do it tonight when we pull up the casket, we can just move the corpse over a bit and shove her in beside the body. Close up the casket and pop it back in the ground. No one will ever find her. And that'll be one less thing to worry about."

"Yeah," Frank said. "Good plan."

"No, it isn't a good plan!" I shouted, eyebrows to my hairline. "A good plan is to let me go on my merry way, and we can all forget this happened."

They ignored me. The guy lifted his chin toward the truck. "Want to grab some zip ties from the tool box? I'll take her to the shack."

Frank loped off, and the guy did some funky move that twisted my wrist backward and locked my elbow. I lost the ability to do anything other than act like a marionette as he pulled my strings, moving me to the shack.

Don't panic, I told myself. *They aren't going to keep an eye on you. You'll be by yourself with time to get out of the predicament.* There was a whole group text full of people who knew where I'd gone. Who might try to respond. When I didn't answer, they'd come looking for me. As long as I'm not yet in the casket, hugging a corpse, they could find me and help me.

I wasn't going to depend on it. Sure, by tomorrow they'd be freaking out and coming after me. But tomorrow would be too late.

"What's your name?" I asked.

"Chris," he said, as he pulled a chair next to the center post and pushed me down.

"That's a nice name." I offered up a friendly smile. "Look, Chris, honestly, this is unnecessary. I couldn't care less what you're up to. Things are tough all over. Sometimes you've got to think outside of the box to get ahead. I respect that in a person. Out of the box thinking." I was doing a lot of out of the box thinking—well, stay out of the casket thinking, anyway. "I applaud you for whatever it is you've got going on. I'm a fan! Go get 'em is what I say." I was clearly babbling. And clearly not shifting the dynamic. "What do you have going? Who's Felicia?"

Frank walked in the door as I said that. "She's jerking your chain. She knew Felicia. They went to school together, and Felicia worked for her at Hooch's. Isn't that right, BJ the bird watcher?"

Okay, so he recognized me. Time to change tactics.

"Why'd you kill Felicia? She obviously cared for you," I said.

"Wasn't me. Chris got a little wound up when Felicia said she wasn't cooperating anymore, that she was going to marry Stewart at the courthouse the next day, and she'd have the money she needed for her mom."

"Did she love Stewart or was that a ruse?" That I really did want to know. I hated to think that Felicia was a gold digger, even if it was for her mom's sake.

Frank looked uncomfortable.

"You came up with a plan that put Felicia with your half-brother, didn't you?"

"Yeah, well, it was a good plan. Felicia and I were seeing each other. Everyone needed money. I knew that he had funeral gigs. I just needed the information—which corpses had jewels and what they were worth. So she went in to get the information."

"As his girlfriend."

He was behind me, reaching forward for my arms and pulled them back awkwardly behind me, the post hitting at my elbows. "Yeah, who knew they'd hit it off? That she'd fall for him. She broke it off with me and accepted a ring from him. Glass." He crossed my wrists to make an X.

"Well, I'm sure if it had been the real thing, you would have stolen it that night."

"Not me, Chris," he said as I felt the plastic looping my wrists. "She wanted out and said that if we gave her any grief she'd turn us in and say we were threatening her for the information."

The band pulled tight around my flesh. "Ouch! No need to be violent about this." I wiggled to try to get some more circulation flowing. "Were you threatening her?" I asked, twisting my head around as far as I could. I wanted to look him in the eye.

"Nah, the threat was her mother's medicines. She'd do just about anything for her mom."

"I can understand that. I'd do the same for my dad. Especially when it really didn't look like anyone was suffering from the crime."

"Exactly. What did you say earlier? No harm, no foul." Frank rose to his feet.

"Until Felicia died," I countered.

"And now you," Frank said.

I looked over at Chris. He shrugged.

"They're blaming the murder on Marley. They're not even looking for you or anyone else. As far as the police go—that's been wrapped up. And me? They will come looking for me. And they will find me. And they will put two and two together. Really, your safest bet is to let me go."

"Yeah, we'll think that over." Frank chuckled and the men left.

They weren't going to think it over. They were going to leave me and then come back and bury me.

That was going to happen over my dead body!

I DIDN'T HEAR a lock tumble when they closed the door. I guessed they assumed I couldn't get free. I was pretty wily, I'd show them!

They stood outside the door, talking in low voices. "What do we do now?" Chris asked.

"I'm going to go search around. BJ isn't the lone-wolf type. Felicia said she and her friend Kay are always together. Chances are she's around here. I just want to make sure she didn't see any of that."

"I'll look this way," Chris answered. "Should I round her up?"

"Nah, if you see Kay, hide."

"You don't think that's a problem?"

"Oh, it's a problem, alright. We just need to nix our plans for tonight and go bury BJ somewhere else. We don't need that kind of headache."

Kay! Thank goodness Kay wasn't here. *She* at least was safe.

The zip cord Frank put around my wrists wasn't the little thin kind that you can pop yourself out of with the right amount of thrust. Well, maybe they were; I couldn't really tell because getting thrust from this position was nigh on impossible. I tried to wiggle my hand out of the restraints, but they were just too darned tight.

I had seen a YouTube video once where a guy used friction from his shoe laces to cut the zip ties off his wrists. But his shoe strings were made of paracord and his hands were in front of his body. If my hands were in front of my body, I bet I could chew through them. In my current state, though, I really couldn't figure a way out. I passed the time sending psychic messages to Connor and Kay. If anyone would pick up on them, it would be them.

THERE WAS movement at the door and I had a nanosecond of hope that Kay had homed in on my SOS signals, gathered the guys, and had come to my rescue.

But then I heard the growl of the dog digger.

The person who came through the door was Frank. *Frank.* I hated that name—it was whiny, like nails scraping down a chalkboard. Thank goodness they had cut the zip ties off. I acted meek and weak. I wanted my despondence to lower their guard as I looked for a chance to get the heck out of there.

If he assumed I had no fight left in me and that I had spent this time coming to grips with my impending doom, maybe he'd make a mistake along the way. I crossed my fingers to boost the juju on that one.

We walked in the light of the tiny pin beam that he had to his flashlight, moving around the statue and back over the hill to Drusilla's grave. There was Chris, lounging in the driver's chair of the dog digger, tipping back a beer. The grass sat to one side of the grave in a nice, neat roll. The earth was mounded on the other side. The flowers and tombstone lay over on the neighboring plot. The elements were all ready to be put back together, no one the wiser, with one new addition. Me.

Frank reached into his pocket, pulled out a casket key, and tossed it to Chris, who stretched out a leisurely arm and snatched it from mid-air.

Chris glugged down his beer and crunched the can into a ball, then tossed it into the grave hole. He jumped down from the cab and stalked the three paces to the grave, put his hand on the ledge, and popped out of sight. The sound of his boots hit the lid with a thump. I leaned to the side.

Six feet under was indeed six feet under.

Now the casket was, I don't know, less than three feet high. When Chris stood, I could see his chest. He walked to the end of the casket and crouched. I heard him grunting, then a rope flew over the side. With me tightly in Frank's grasp, we moved to the rope. Chris put both hands on the side of the grave and pushed his weight up while Frank stooped to grab the rope.

Now was my chance. I side-kicked his knee sending him sprawling into the grave. But he didn't let me go.

I threw my arm wide, trying to catch myself, and caught my fingers on Chris's belt and clung on tight. With Frank's and my weight and momentum, Chris came crashing down into the grave with us. The flashlight stayed topside.

The three of us were in a tangle. I was clawing and biting and scrambling. I got my foot on someone's something and launched myself over the lip. I sprawled onto the grass, bent at the hip with my legs dangling into the opening and my fingers clawing the grass for leverage.

I kicked my legs furiously to stop either man from getting a good hold on me. I was screaming my head off. With a new burst of adrenaline, I got all the way out of the hole and crawled forward. As I pushed to standing, a steel grasp encircled my ankle. There was a blur of movement and then another scream.

Not mine.

A manly scream. Well, manly was a stretch.

My ankle slipped from the grasp. I flipped over onto my butt to crab-walk backward, away from the hellhole.

The beam of a flashlight caught on the black fur of

Twinkles the Wonder Dog. His white fangs gleamed in the light. He ground his teeth into Frank's arm. Chris launched himself out the other side of the hole and took off running. I heard an OOF! As he went crashing to the ground.

More flashlights.

More movement.

Kay knelt onto the ground beside me and wrapped me in her arms. Rocking me like I was a baby, petting my hair.

Someone flipped on the dog digger lights and the whole scene came to life.

Connor had his knee on Frank's back as he wrenched the guy's arms into handcuffs.

Johnson walked Chris away from the scene; he was already in cuffs.

Dick had both hands wrapped in Twinkles's collar as he snarled and leapt at the men.

Sirens shrilled up the street and I saw a fire truck, an ambulance, and backup cop cars all roaring into place.

Nick of damn time.

DAD WAS GIVING me the stink eye from where he stood with his crew. They had given me the once over, but he wanted to hear my explanation for why I was wrestling around in a dug up grave- bizarro scene he had rolled up on. He hadn't known it was me when Dick had called it in. It didn't take them long to get help in place; the stations weren't but a few blocks down the road.

I started at the beginning and laid the story out as best I could. It wasn't like Chris told me the exact how and why of Felicia's death, just that she was done being a criminal, and she actually really did have feelings for Stewart. Then I launched breathlessly into how I got caught after I'd sent the video, and how grateful I was that they had arrived when they did.

Everyone stood in silence while the backup cops moved Chris and Frank to the cars and headed toward the jail. Twinkles stopped growling, and Dick let go of his collar so he could trot, tail wagging, over and sit in my lap. The big fur baby.

"Does this mean they'll let Marley go?" I asked Connor.

"It's not as easy as that. We'll have to see what the Commonwealth's Attorney says in the morning. I can't imagine them keeping him, though. We'll need you to come down and make a statement."

Dad leaned forward. "I think she needs to go to the hospital for a once over."

"I'm fine. Some bruising and stuff from the zip ties. No big deal."

"No big deal?" Kay, Connor, and Dad said in unison.

"Okay, big deal. But I'm not hurt. I'm fine." Then, to change the subject, "How did you find me?"

"I'd been scared for you since you sent me the video. I called you over and over, but my calls just went to voicemail. I went to your apartment and Twinkles was starving and needed a walk, so I knew something was wrong." She pointed over to the side by the tree, where Terrance was standing.

He gave me a little wave.

"Terrance and I brought Twinkles with us to Hooch's. The door was locked, but you have a new citation taped to the door."

"Awesome," I said sarcastically. Tonight? Go ahead and tape citations to my door. I was alive to read them. Go me!

"I called Connor," Kay said. "Connor called Dick and

Johnson, since they were the other two people in your group text, and we all converged at the bar to figure out what might have happened."

"I did a Google 'find my phone'," Connor said. "Since I know your passwords, and it said you were over on this side of the cemetery. We all headed over here and Kay told Twinkles to find Mommy. That's when we heard the screaming."

"Yeah," I said, "seemed like the right thing to do."

There were silent nods. The EMS packed up their things to go. Dad came over to give me a hug.

Suddenly a breeze blew by and Twinkles stuck his nose in the air. He took off down the hill.

"Where's he going?" Connor asked.

I scrambled to chase after him. "If he thinks I'm going to let him eat any more of that unicorn poop, he is *shit* out of luck."

Yup. I was pretty darned sure I'd used up our family's luck quota for today.

THE SERIES CONTINUES ...

IF YOU SEE KAY ...

The series continues with
IF YOU SEE KAY FREEZE.
Coming Soon!
And don't forget to check
out BJ & Kay's first adventure
in IF YOU SEE KAY RUN.

ALSO BY THE AUTHORS

Also by Fiona:

The Lynx Series
That Which is Yours
Weakest Lynx
Missing Lynx
Chain Lynx
Cuff Lynx

Strike Force
In Too DEEP
JACK Be Quick

Uncommon Enemies
WASP
RELIC
DEADLOCK

Kate Hamilton Mysteries

Mine
Yours

Also by Tina:

Spark Before Dying Series
Deadly Sins
Angels Cry
Burden of Proof

Det. Damien Scott Series
When the Devil Takes Hold
Sticks & Stones
Foul Play

STAY IN TOUCH WITH US!

Glasneck & Quinn - Brew Ho Ho

Connect with Fiona Quinn at www.FionaQuinnBooks.com
Also:
@FionaQuinnBooks on Twitter
Fiona Quinn Books on Facebook
Fiona Quinn Books on Pinterest

Connect with Tina Glasneck:
I enjoy connecting with my readers. Send me an email,Tina@TinaGlasneck [dot] com, and I promise to respond!

Join my newsletter, connect with me on Facebook, and never miss a release, as well!

DID YOU ENJOY IF YOU SEE KAY HIDE?

Recommend it:

Please help others find this great story by recommending it. You can also recommend it by posting about it on your social media sites, like Twitter and Facebook.

Review it:

Please tell others why you liked this book. You can review it where books are sold, and in your online reading communities.

ACKNOWLEDGMENTS

We'd like to acknowledge our editor, Lindsay Smith, and our cover artist Chandell Aikman Sites, for their hard work, dedication, and professionalism. Thank you ladies for helping to make this jewel shine.

To our beta readers and our street team members, thank you for your support, enthusiasm, and excellent feedback. You all rock, and your words of encouragement, future marketing plans and jokes helped this to be a wonderful experience.

To all the wonderful professionals who helped us get the details right, especially our local law enforcement, who provided the Citizen's Police Academy. Please note in fiction, while we try our best to get the details right, we have not committed any crimes, so in the end we had to make some stuff up. Please understand that any discrepancies come from our authorial decision making, and rest squarely on our shoulders.

We've never actually observed unicorns in the wild, but if you do happen to see them, let us know.

Also, we went to great lengths regarding dogs and marshmallows. We are not advocating the feeding of any pet marshmallows in the hope that they will poop out jewels.

Made in the USA
Columbia, SC
16 October 2017